Scars Like Wings

A FAIRY TALE LIFE
BOOK 4

C. B. STAGG

Scars Like Wings

ISBN-13: 978-1979045988

Cover designed C. B. Stagg

Formatting by C. B. Stagg

Edited by Christina M. Scambray

A Note to Readers

Book four? It doesn't even seem possible. I started this journey thirteen months ago, hoping to cross *Publish Novel* off my 'Before 40' bucket list! And here we are! If you're here, that means you've read the first three books in the Fairy Tale Life series (if not, this book may not make complete sense, so please read them first!). The plan right now is to end this series at book 6, but you know what they say about the best-laid plans…

As an independently published author, the greatest gift you can give me is reading my book. The second greatest gift is reviewing the book on Amazon, B&N, or where ever you purchased it. Authors like me rely heavily on reviews to keep getting our books into the hands of readers like you. If you're reading this on Kindle, just keep flipping to the very last page and you'll have an opportunity to review the book right there while it's fresh in your mind!

Also, follow me on Amazon, Facebook, check out my Instagram, take a peek at my website. There are so many more stories I have to tell, so don't miss out on a release!

Yours, Charly Stagg

http://www.cbstaggauthor.com @CBStaggAuthor

Available Now:

An Ordinary Fairy Tale (A Fairy Tale Life Book #1)

If Wishes Were Horses (A Fairy Tale Life Book #2)

Five Minutes to Midnight (A Fairy Tale Life Book #3)

Scars Like Wings (A Fairy Tale Life Book #4)

Coming Soon:

Life on the Ground (A Fairy Tale Life Book #5)

To my family...
I love you more
than anything else
in the world!

She conquered
her demons,
and wore her

Scars
Like
Wings.
-Atticus

Prologue

Bennett

I'D SEEN THIS GODFORSAKEN desert through a vast array of lenses during my short tour of Iraq. From a dark amber lens combatting the unforgiving sun, to protective goggles scuffed to near opaqueness while handling explosives, to night vision when the threat of an invisible enemy loomed in the shadows of darkness. But the pink hue coating the visor of my helmet was not one of optimism and positivity, which are so often associated with a rose-colored tint. No, the slick veil of blood spatter marring my vision revealed the desert for what it truly was: an evil hothouse with dust demons dancing on the scorched terrain. The armpit of Satan himself.

It was Hell on Earth.

"The trauma pack! Get the trauma pack!"

A man with an American accent fired back and forth with a staticky radio voice. Damn! Was our convoy hit or was his distress call for someone else? The man mumbled like he had a mouth full of cotton balls, preventing further comprehension on my part. I hoped the sorry SOB on the other end understood what he was trying to tell them. The tone behind his words sent chills down my spine. I know panic and unadulterated fear when I hear it, but fear or not, the persistent ringing in my head made everything sound like I was a million miles away.

Any attempt to wipe my eyes was futile. Hard as I tried, nothing was happening. My arm lay at my side like a sleeping dog. Move, damn it! The only things cooperating were my eyes. But even then, they were next to useless. My eyelids were wet and sticky. When I blinked, they stuck together like soggy postage stamps. Everything was clingy, bonding to the closest object, cemented by some unknown substance.

But I was falling apart at the seams. I struggled to see, to move, even to draw a breath. I felt high, like that one time in high school I'd eaten a friend's 'special' brownies, going back for seconds and thirds before I knew things weren't right. Something in my brain wasn't connecting with the rest of my body. *What we have here is a failure to communicate.* The words from *Cool Hand Luke* fluttered in and out of my semiconscious, yet panic-stricken mind.

Mercifully, I shook free from the confines of my bucket and was better able to assess the situation. Part of my problem was the 250 pounds of solid muscle pinning me to the hot, dry land.

"Off!" I screamed, though the voice didn't carry the

weight of a US Army sergeant. It was more like a choked whisper… my pathetic attempt at authority. "Now." I tried again, getting the same result.

"Sgt. Hanson? That you?" The question tumbled from his lips and the tremor in the voice put me on high alert. Panic. More panic. The disembodied call came from somewhere above me, but I didn't have the neck strength or inclination to identify the man behind the words. His accent was American, which provided a sliver of relief to my growing anxiety.

The voice leaned down into my face.

Commander Daniels.

The man had been with Chance and me since Day One and was like a father to me. He was career army and had to be the most intelligent man I knew. He said he saw himself when he looked at me, a compliment I found equally flattering and terrifying. But this wasn't the man I knew. Fear radiated from his eyes, and his hands shook so violently he struggled to operate the radio in his hands.

"You okay, Commander?" I had to ask. He was paper white. His knees buckled and he landed on the ground beside me. It tore me up to watch a man I had such great respect for—one I looked up to and emulated—topple over like a house of cards.

"Yeah, I need to check on my squad." The old horse cavalry rules kicked in. Feed your horses, your men, and yourself. In that order.

"Let me just... " He scuttled away, calling to someone behind him, his command unintelligible. Were these men poor communicators or was it me? Everything sounded like it was happening under water.

Several pairs of dusty, black boots shuffled uncomfortably close to my face, but they did manage to lift him off—the soldier and the person who knew my best and my worst—from my chest. I choked down steamy air and a fair amount of sand, trying to replenish my oxygen supply as the men placed him on the ground a few feet away. It was hard for me to get a good look, but even using only my peripheral vision, it was clear something was terribly wrong.

"Chance?" In my head, I already knew it was him, but now I was sure. His body, or what was left of it, sat awkwardly wadded up like a piece of discarded paper. Most of one leg appeared to be missing and the other was gone altogether. A river of thick, metallic-smelling plasma flowed through angry vessels, pumping from a jagged hole in his torso with surprising force. Blood and flesh covered the ground. I reached out to touch him, ignoring the flaming stabs of pain shooting through my body as I moved. With tremendous effort, I was able to scoot close enough to reach his hand with the tip of my finger.

The wind picked up and sand started flying around, swarming like angry wasps. The unmistakable sound of helicopters followed and before I could blink, I was surrounded once again by grimy boots coming at me from all angles. With every ounce of energy I had, I lunged to say goodbye to my friend. When I squeezed his hand with a painful finality—one last contact between brothers—something slipped from his grip. I didn't even have to look to know what it was. Chance's most treasured possession, his good luck charm. The fact that it was the last thing in his hands before he died was an irony not lost on me. I swiped the small, worn photo from the blood-soaked desert floor before it could blow away, grasping it as if my life depended on it.

Moments, or maybe hours, later, I was carried off on a makeshift stretcher and loaded onto the first of three, possibly four, helicopters waiting beyond the dunes. Taking one last look at the destruction that had been our convoy—on a simple mission to pick up supplies from Camp Doha—I could see the puddle of blood where I'd lain seconds before. *Was all that mine?*

Chance's body had already been loaded into one of the other choppers; one used for cargo, not medical transport. He was gone. With that realization, the adrenaline formerly blocking the reality of my condition seeped away. From somewhere deep within my defeated soul, a guttural scream emerged before my mind took control. The scene before me, worthy of a Wes Craven film, faded into darkness… but not before one small detail was seared into my mind. Amidst the puddle of blood, now mixing with the sand to create an ominous, rusty-red mud, one thing remained. The blistering wasteland of that vile Middle Eastern desert took a souvenir from the United States Army. *Still* dressed in desert camo, with the black combat boot *still* laced up and tied as if it had been done just seconds before, lay half a leg—perfectly intact, owner yet to be determined.

Chapter 1

Jillian

"STATE OF TEXAS vs. Jillian Walker, case number 85-0492-DT-510."

Judge Norma Jean Kirby (yes, she uses both names) pushed her glasses up onto her long, narrow nose as her ancient bailiff shuffled back to his designated area. The judge herself resembled an ostrich, with large, oversized marble eyes and feathery grey hair cropped short against her head. She showed more scalp than was acceptable for a woman, only adding to her bird-like appearance.

Her long, thin neck, extending from her judicial robes, was in need of an iron, reminding me of something my mother always says: *Nothing reveals age quicker than the neck and the hands.* She could easily add female baldness to that list, I thought, then snorted. I covered the faux pas with a cough.

"Ms. Walker, I have been provided paperwork stating that you and the state have come to an agreement with respect to how the allegations being brought against you will be handled. Is that your understanding?"

"Yes, Your Honor." I'd worn a demure, grey pantsuit with a light pink silk shell beneath the fitted jacket. The string of Mikimoto freshwater pearls, a gift from my parents for my sixteenth birthday three years earlier, were a last minute addition to my ensemble. My frosted blonde hair, neatly pulled back away from my face, drew attention to the one-carat diamond earrings Daddy had brought to the hospital just a few weeks earlier. They were meant to make me feel better about what he referred to as 'my unfortunate ordeal.' And they had.

"Do you understand that the allegation is driving while intoxicated?"

"Yes, Your Honor." I kept my voice even, unemotional, and my face devoid of expression. *Contrite* is the word our family attorney, Jamison, used. While tediously preparing for this trial he used that word, along with *remorseful, humble,* and *apologetic. Virginal* may have been thrown in there too, though I can't really remember. The fact was, my father paid him a higher end, six-figure salary to create an illusion of sophisticated innocence. What neither of them realized was—between my years of cotillion, finishing school, state dinners, and even my recent summer internship at the capitol—I was bred for this. It was in my blood. I had this thing in the bag.

"This charge carries with it a potential incarceration

of 180 days in jail, do you understand that?"

"Yes, Your Honor." Perspiration was starting to affect my grip on the handles of the god-awful walker I'd be forced to rely on for the foreseeable future. I had to admit, though, it was a hell of a lot better than the wheelchair I'd been relegated to up until only a few days ago. *How much longer, people?* We'd hammered out all the details with the district attorney's office weeks ago. This was some kind of *deja vu* hell.

"The paperwork I have been given tells me the proposed resolution is that you be admitted into what is called a *pretrial diversion program.* As a result, there will be no plea and there will be no actual charges brought against you... *at this time.*" Those last three staccato words fired from her sickly thin lips like bullets. "Is this clear?"

"Yes, ma'am." *Your natural face is sour lemons, Jillian. You must always smile.* With my mother's words echoing in my subconscious, I did what I was taught to do in a public setting; *smile with the bottom half of my face, so as not to look overly impressed or excited. Never let the smile cause your eyes to wrinkle.* I was good at this. I went through the majority of my life in just this manner.

What a colossal waste of my time. *Yes,* I understood I was not being charged. *Of course,* I understood I would never serve time. My father *was* Harrison Walker. Former representative and now governor of the great state of Georgia, eyeing the presidential seat once

Bush's term was up. There was no way I would be charged or whatever. In a matter of months, weeks maybe, this little incident would be just a tiny hiccup in my otherwise perfect life. I glanced down at my new diamond-encrusted Tag Heuer to check the time.

"So, he explained you have the right to a trial and by signing this agreement, you are waiving that right. However, you also understand, the state still reserves the right to file a case against you if you fail to meet the terms laid out in the contract. Am I correct in assuming this?" My head snapped up to meet the disapproving eyes of the judge. Damn.

I nodded once more, biting the inside of my cheek to keep my eyes from rolling back into my head. She shook her head slowly. Judges made decent money, didn't they? One would think she'd have all that extra skin on her neck nipped and tucked. It was distracting. My mother knew a guy. Hell, she had her own parking space at her plastic surgeon's office in Atlanta.

She turned to speak to her bailiff and I shuffled in place, a grimace temporarily replacing the pleased expression I'd had plastered on my face for going on half an hour. My pain meds were wearing off, and the painful pressure that standing so long was putting on my midsection was building like a siren. I was becoming increasingly grateful my attorney had insisted on flats instead of the stilettos (purchased in France from new designer Louboutin) I'd originally chosen as the crowning jewel of my courtroom attire.

4

"Now that these charges are *formally* on record, you need to be notified *formally* of the charges being brought against you."

This again? Really? It's a done deal, lady!

This backroom deal had been made before my sweet little BMW Z1 Roadster had even been towed away from the accident site. I'm sure my father never anticipated my having to stand at the defense table with a broken pelvis, while some queen of the boondocks county judge made me relive one of the less than stellar moments of my life over and over.

The portly and poorly dressed assistant district attorney stood from the table where he'd been slumped in an uncomfortable chair that looked to be circa 1940, and lumbered toward me. From what I could see out of the corner of my eye, I was relatively certain he'd been working the New York Times crossword puzzle while Judge Turkey Neck droned on and on.

"Can you please state your name for the record?" His voice was much too high for his bloated body and he was sweating profusely. My disgust turned to relief when he stopped a few feet from the table where I stood, placing me just out of his perspiration splash zone.

"Jillian Walker, sir." That *sir* at the end was to show respect, of which I had none.

"Ms. Walker, you are being charged with driving

while intoxicated, an incident occurring on April 1, 1992. I am asking your attorney to acknowledge this accusation, waiving a more formal reading, and enter a plea for the record."

"We acknowledge the reading and we enter a plea of not guilty." Jamison patted me on the back, causing my shirt to stick to my skin where he made contact. The month of May in Texas wasn't exactly known for its pleasant weather, but the room was cool. I, on the other hand, was not. The pain was becoming unbearable.

"Your Honor," the mealy DA addressed the judge, who now appeared about as bored as the rest of us. "The defendant has been accepted into the DIVERT program and we are in agreement with that decision, assuming the following conditions." He mopped his forehead with a handkerchief he'd retrieved from his back pocket and focused his beady eyes on mine.

"Pretrial Diversion will be for a term of 18 months, and will require community service and drug and alcohol conditions."

Community service? Was he kidding?

"But I was told I could pay a fine!" I shrieked. My momentary loss of control earned a stern look from Jamison and I popped my pleasant smile back into its place.

"And based on a prior *inadmissible* charge, the state

6

also requires Ms. Walker only drive to and from school and community service and she may not be on the roads between the hours of ten p.m. and six a.m."

Excuse me, what? Seems if that little misstep from last year was inadmissible… it would be *inadmissible*… but here it is, being *admitted*. This wasn't part of the plan either.

Not liking being caught off guard, Jamison's hackles rose and he moved in closer to the DA, letting his proximity and intimidating size betray the syrupy, Southern drawl he'd been using to charm the court.

"Now, let's stop for just a minute here." He closed his portfolio and strolled into the empty space separating the judge from the accused. "I think it's important to mention, Ms. Walker has been an active member of her community, both here in College Station during her time at Texas A&M University and back home in Savannah. She was a model student at her high school in Georgia, maintaining a 4.0 average all four years, and likewise, has been no less impressive while attending school in Texas." Yeah. One would think my position as Director of Philanthropy within my sorority would count for something.

"She comes from a well-known family, and they have high expectations for her future. Surely, Your Honor, as you can see, this is merely one bad decision made by a respectable young lady with a bright future ahead of her."

Judge Kirby was leaning over the bench, her glasses resting on the tip of her beak as she pinned him with a glare of epic proportions. Her penciled-on eyebrows had long disappeared into her thinning hairline, making the wrinkles marking her face even more severe than when it was at rest. It didn't appear his Southern charm worked on bitter old hags with Northern accents.

"I have read the entire pretrial packet, *Mister* Jamison. I am well-aware of Ms. Walker's *character*." Her sarcasm was unnerving. "In addition, I have read the full report, all responses to those reports, and while I may not understand or agree with this resolution, I respect the decision of the State."

Then, I found *myself* the recipient of said glare. "The fact you've been admitted into the DIVERT program is no guarantee you'll complete the program, you do understand this, Ms. Walker?"

"Yes, Your Honor." My hands shook.

"And the person responsible for the completion of this program, ultimately, is you. Are we clear?"

My stomach rolled like thunder, not at her words, but at the pain shooting through my body. A quick nod acknowledged her question, and Jamison wrapped his arm around me, easing my body down into a chair, seconds before I would've melted onto the cold tile floor. My body had had enough. When documents were signed and hands were shaken, I stood, with help, just as the judge called out.

"Mr. Jamison, I'd like to address your client personally." Pain meds were officially out of my system and I worried if I didn't lie down soon, I'd find myself in the ER. But I soldiered on, standing a little taller as I faced the old woman.

"Ms. Walker, I'll put it to you plainly. I think you are a spoiled brat. Your family's relationship with our state's governor and your father's political influence are the main reasons you aren't serving time for such reckless endangerment… coupled with the fact that it was a single vehicle accident… *and* I have no doubt you'll be suffering the consequences of your choices in the weeks, months, and even years to come." She stood. The legs of her chair scraped the floor, creating a screech I'd imagine coming from the throat of a pterodactyl.

"This time, Daddy was able to swoop in and save you. But if you're not careful, there will come a day when you find yourself in a mess that even your father's long arms can't reach. I hope you will view this as the second chance it is and take full advantage. It's time for you to get your life on track." She was tall… incredibly tall. And given the judge's bench already stood a good four feet above everything else, I strained my neck to maintain eye contact. I'm sure this was part of her scare tactic.

"You need to see how the other half live. Then, maybe you'll learn to appreciate what you have. I want you out in the field, serving the people of this community, and I know just the place for you to do it. I want you to push yourself, get out of your comfort zone, get your hands dirty. And when your time is up, I'd like to see you again."

The feeling was most definitely *not mutual*.

"I know this might be a bitter pill to swallow, but I think it is the best medicine when it comes to someone like you. So, I order you to come back here when you've finished your community service and prove me right. Don't make me regret allowing you to leave my court without more than this pathetic attempt at a slap on the wrist."

Chapter 2

Bennett

May 30, 1992

SEEING LANDSTUHL REGIONAL Medical Center in the rearview mirror of my transport Humvee was a balm on my bruised and battered spirit. Yes, it was an American hospital. Yes, the majority of the staff spoke English and were very hospitable. But the simple fact was, it was in Germany. I needed American air, American sun, American soil. I needed baseball, apple pie, and the good old red, white, and blue. I needed home, and in less than an hour's time, that's exactly where I'd be headed.

I double-checked my rucksack, containing everything I physically owned in this world. A few sets of BDUs and a bag of toiletries occupied the main compartment. In the front, there was a folder containing the contract from the bank, signed and ready to be mailed when I was stateside, and the college admission letter I had yet to respond to.

My passport was there, along with my now-expired driver's license, both tucked securely in the side pocket.

The newspaper I'd smuggled out of the occupational therapy waiting room that morning—old and out-of-date, but no less valuable—was sticking out from the top of my bag where I'd stashed it before leaving for the air base. And in my pants pocket, Chance's wrecked picture. His beauty. His golden girl. But I knew that already. I'd checked for it no less than ten times on the drive to the plane, but I checked again. Everything else was replaceable. *She* was not.

We boarded the aircraft with little fanfare. I wondered if I'd miss the cocktail of the spicy scent of baharat, cheap aftershave, and sweat when I got home. Probably not.

My plan was to kick back, relax, and make the most of my twenty-four-hour flight to DC by getting up to speed on the happenings of the Western world. I'd only been gone just shy of two years: four months lying in wait on the Saudi border, two months falling apart on the battlefield, and fifteen months putting myself back together, mind and body, though neither would ever be the same. War felt like a lifetime. And the way I'd gone about it? Ten lifetimes.

"Where ya headed, once we land?" I pulled my hand from my pocket, where I'd been holding the picture, and ran it through my already sweat-damp hair. Why did I always feel like a naughty child getting caught with his hand in the cookie jar when I held Chance's girl? Probably because she was just that: Chance's girl. For the thousandth time, I wondered if I should have let her die with him on the desert floor turned battlefield. But that's not what he would've wanted. Chance was my best friend, my brother in that hole. He would have laid his life down for his golden girl just like he did for me, so it was *my* responsibility to keep her safe. Because he no longer could.

"This is it, right here Ben. This is why I'm here." Chance's philosophical moods were exhausting, but he put up with my grumpy ass, so I owed it to him to listen to his musings. The two of us met at basic, but only became friends during our time in Saudi, holding at Dharan while we awaited orders.

"You talk about 'this' all the time brother, though you never let me in on what 'this' is." I attempted to sound perturbed, but my smile was always evident in my voice. At least, that's what Rosie always told me.

"You're right, asshole. And you'll never know." I rolled my eyes. I'd looked over his shoulder a time or two and knew it was a picture of three people perched on the edge of a stone wall, arms thrown around each other. I hadn't seen it up close, but there was only one thing that could make a soldier smile like that—a girl."

"Who is she?" I decided to take a chance, see if he'd take the bait.

"No one." His words were meant for me, but his gaze never left hers. *"It doesn't matter. It isn't like that. She's like a sister."* He sighed, but I don't think he was even aware of

it.

"Well, I can't speak from experience since I never had a sister, but if I did… and I spent as much time looking at her as you do looking at yours… I'd need to visit a psychologist."

Chance shook his head and tucked the picture back into his left pocket. "The sister thing is her choice, not mine." Ah, so there's the truth. Unrequited love.

"Maybe things will change when you get home." My friend swung his legs over the side of his cot and stood, stretching high in the air.

"Nope. By the time I get home, she'll be married." With that he walked toward the smell of food, but just like always, his left hand was in his pocket, no doubt holding on to something that would never be, both literally and figuratively.

"Hello? Earth to Hanson." I shook myself back into the present, coming face-to-face with one of the biggest grins that ever joined the army. I cleared the vision from my mind as I checked my pocket again. "Where'd you go just now? Or do I even want to know?"

Botts, or Biscuit, as he liked to be called, was a buddy from my time in Germany. I met him shortly after the incident. He'd lost a few toes from his right foot, a couple fingers from his left hand, and his hearing on one side. His occupational therapy happened at the same time I was in physical therapy. With little else to do there, we struck up a conversation one day and the rest was history.

He went by Biscuit because he said if he could have anything in the world from back home, it would be his momma's biscuits and gravy. I could think of a million other things I wanted and none of them would be food, so his momma must make some damn fine biscuits. Maybe he'd invite me over for some once we were stateside.

We only spoke in present tense, never past and never future. That's the funny thing about the army. We kept all conversations superficial. Talking about the past was too painful. Most guys left something behind; a mom and dad, little brothers and sisters, a girlfriend, maybe even a wife and kids for some of the older guys. Mail deliveries, for me, were a double-edged sword. On one hand, it made me smile to see my buddies get letters and packages from home. On the other, I always left empty-handed.

We didn't speak of the future either, not really. Sure, we'd talk about going to a baseball game, or eating real food again. It was fine to daydream out loud, but we didn't talk about our future selves. At least I didn't. While I wouldn't refer to myself as superstitious, something in the back of my mind told me speaking of the future was a guarantee I wouldn't have one. Counting your chickens before they hatch and all that crap. I needed to put some honest-to-goodness thought in about my future. I'd get right on it once I was safe in the States.

Neither Biscuit nor I wanted to admit the men we'd been before were long gone. It was much easier trying to figure out which nurses were sleeping with which doctors. No, I didn't know too much about the man outside of the hospital walls and didn't care to learn at this point. But he definitely wasn't a fan of silence, so he chose to fill it with meaningless chatter.

"Where're ya headed from here? We're out now. There's a light at the end of the tunnel. You can tell me now without jinxing anything."

"Don't know really." That was a lie. I did know, but I wasn't quite ready to speak of it. Based on his wide eyes and gaping jaw, one would think I'd told him I was headed right on out to strangle stray cats.

"Whattaya mean, ya don't know? Surely ya got a woman or a family? That's where ya go, man. Home isn't the USA, home is where your people are. You got people, right Hanson?" He was so touchy-feely. Me, not so much.

Elbow me one more time, pal.

"Well, I think I might just go to Texas." My intent was to deflect his question, but in hindsight, my answer reflected what was truly in my heart. He slapped me on the back.

"Who's in Texas?"

I shook my head. "It's not *who*, it's *what*. I think I might go to college." There it was. I'd said it out loud, that was as good as a commitment. I'd applied months ago, and just a week ago received word at least one school had accepted me and it only took one. I wasn't picky.

"That's what I'm talkin' 'bout, man. That's what I'm talkin' 'bout."

Time to switch to plan B, to feign sleep for the eternal flight to DC. Screw the Western world. I still had another three-hour flight from DC to Houston. We could become reacquainted then.

Maybe.

"Hey, Biscuit. Where're you headed again?" I was all shared out. I needed peace on my flight to Houston.

"Aw, Savannah, man. My people're in Georgia."

Satisfied I'd be parting ways with Biscuit's big mouth and sharp elbows, I handed him the paper, settled in, and prepared for takeoff. Once I flew into Houston Intercontinental Airport and my feet hit the pavement, I had no immediate plan as to where I'd go first or what I'd do, but those things hardly mattered.

I was going home.

Fall, 1992

Chapter 3

Bennett

ONE WOULD THINK AFTER months and months in the desert with limited air conditioning, I'd be used to the heat... but there was something about Texas heat that outranked all others in its level of severity. The one hundred degree temperatures—combined with the intense humidity—created nature's very own sauna. It was impossible to even walk the short distance from the library to the counseling office without some major sweat rings. Oh well, at least I knew I wouldn't be the only one.

"Well, from what I see here, everything's in order." I'd been sitting in the office of Mrs. Lillie Lowe, a short African-American woman with mahogany skin and hair slightly graying at her temples, for close to thirty minutes as she carefully combed through each one of the eight million forms I'd filled out since being accepted. Mrs. Lowe was my newly assigned academic advisor and the only soul I knew within a hundred-mile radius.

"All I need is for you to sign and date at the bottom

here, and you'll be all ready to go." She handed me a black Bic pen and shuffled the papers in my direction with a soft smile. "And just in time, too. Classes start tomorrow, you know."

"Yes, ma'am." I paused, pen hovering over where X marks the spot. "Hey, I'm sorry about all this." I murmured, scrawling my name on the dotted line, finalizing this new path my life would take. "Nothing like waiting 'til the last minute, huh?" I tried to smile as I handed the form back, partly to charm the old woman in front of me, and partly to curb the growing dread in my stomach.

"Why psychology, may I ask?"

That was a loaded question. Was it because I was a good listener? Yes, I *was* that. I'd proven it time and time again at Landstuhl. Helping soldiers work through anything from the death of a buddy, the loss of a limb, to survivor's guilt... I was the guy they came to between mandated appointments with their assigned shrinks.

They said talking about all their crap with a friend was easier on their pride. I was approachable, not clinical. I had no official say in anything, so they felt comfortable opening up, like two friends meeting for a beer at the neighborhood bar. It got to the point where the counselors, psychiatrists, and I would work together on particularly difficult cases. They said I had a gift. I say I was just using the problems of others to mask my own. Either way, it brought me here.

"I want to better understand the human mind." It was a BS answer, but until I knew her better that was all she was getting. Her smile said it was enough. For now.

Because I'd decided to try my hand at college only recently, and this poor woman drew the short straw, I allowed her a limited amount of time to get everything in order. Honestly, she must have some hidden magic wand because I was shocked when she said I wouldn't have to sit out this semester. She'd been a saint through the process of selecting a path, registering for classes... not to mention holding my hand through the financial aid process. I was attending Texas A&M University on the GI Bill, which meant dealing with the military. That was no easy task.

"Mrs. Lowe, I can't thank you enough for all you've done." I sat back in the uncomfortable maroon leather chair, one of two that sat in the too small, ground floor office. It was a spot I'd occupied many times since arriving in College Station only a week before. The day after I had things squared away at the ranch I'd just sunk my entire life savings into, I was college-bound.

I'd chosen Texas A&M for two reasons. One, it's where Doc, my foster father, was an Aggie. He graduated with a Bachelor of Science in Animal Husbandry back in the sixties and it was Doc who told me college was even an option. He believed in me, had no problem saying so, and I was ready to make him proud. Second, it was the only college in which I was accepted. Since they wanted me, I wanted them.

Mrs. Lowe stood and walked out from behind her hulking desk to stand by the window. Looking out, I saw what caught her attention; a pair of squirrels chased each other up and down one of the large oak trees shading much of the campus.

"I usually don't share much about myself with my students, Mr. Hanson, but I feel like today might be a good day to change that." I stood and moved closer to her. She'd spent an exponential amount of time on me the last several days, the least I could do was give the woman my complete and undivided attention.

"I had a son who would be about your age right now. He was in the army and was one of the first casualties of Operation Desert Shield. Bridge bombing. Wrong place, wrong time, I guess." She shrugged her narrow shoulders. The range of emotions crossing her face as she spoke said she was probably reconstructing what happened over there, a dangerous and unproductive train of thought for soldiers and their families. Imaginations could be a powerful weapon, especially when used to attack ourselves.

She sighed deep, letting the air out slowly, saying goodbye to her memories and coming back to the present. "I usually handle the end of the alphabet, but when your case popped up, I asked for it." Her arms were wrapped tight across her chest and she appeared to be talking to the squirrels. She shrugged again, and turned to face me, taking another deep breath. "There wasn't much I could do to help my son, Bennett, but I can help you."

"I'm very sorry for your loss, ma'am." I sat back down. Keeping my eyes on her, she settled herself in the chair next to me.

"I am, too. Believe me." She smiled with the lower half of her face, but in her eyes lived a sadness I hadn't noticed before. "A minute ago, you mentioned thanking me."

I nodded. "Yes, ma'am."

"Well, work hard, study, make good grades. Then, go out into the world and make a difference. Do the things my son will never have the opportunity to do. That's all the thanks I need." I handed her a tissue from the box on her desk and she dashed away the few tears rolling down her cheeks.

"I can do that, Mrs. Lowe." I stood and she followed, collecting the papers with my schedule and other important pieces of information. Sliding them into a manila file folder, she pressed it into my hands.

"Any luck with finding an apartment yet? I noticed we're still using your campus PO Box as your residence, but I'll need to replace it with a physical address soon."

I shook my head, keeping it down. "No, ma'am. Not yet, but I'm working on it." But was I? No, not really. I hadn't let myself believe any of this was actually happening until this very moment. It was only when I saw my full name at the top of an actual academic schedule I finally realized I would have a reason to stay in town.

"Bennett, do you need help? I could—"

"No, ma'am, finding a place to rest my head is now my number one priority. I'll get on it right away."

"Well, okay then… " She didn't believe me, that much was clear. "Here," She grabbed a card from her desk and shoved it into my hand. One side was a map. On the other, an address. "And grab a few of those apples from the basket on the way out. You're hungry. Don't think I didn't hear that stomach of yours rumbling. I had to look out the window to see if a storm was rolling in, it was so loud."

I laughed. It felt good to have someone fussing over me again. After four years in the army, Lillie Lowe's deep, warm voice was a nice change from the clipped, dry communication style of the military. She reminded me of Doc's wife.

Foster care made me feel invisible, like I wasn't even worth looking at. But once I landed at the ranch, everything changed. Rosie, my foster mom, fussed something awful… but even with all the eye-rolling attitude I handed her for it, she knew I loved her as much as she loved me. She and Doc always knew exactly what I needed and in the three years I was placed with them, I thrived.

"I'll see you soon, then?" I nodded as she opened the door and ushered me out into the small, stuffy lobby. It was packed, students filling every chair and most of the floor space. *Were they all waiting to see her?* I did not envy that woman, but I had faith she'd handle it all with grace.

"Go to the first floor circulation desk at the main library. My husband is in charge over there. He can help you find books to get you started and I expect you to check in with me toward the end of the week, you hear?" I wanted to reply, *Yes, Mom,* but held my tongue, given the sad story she'd just shared.

"Miss Walker, come on in." She was signaling to someone over my shoulder, already moving on to the next fire she had to extinguish. As I grabbed a few apples, shoving them into the pockets of my cargo pants, before grabbing a few more, a beautiful blonde brushed past me and into Mrs. Lowe's office.

The air surrounding her smelled like vanilla and girl. She plopped down in the seat I'd just vacated, but not before giving me a pinched face glare, making it clear I couldn't even afford to breathe her vanilla-scented air. I shrugged, taking a noisy bite of a green apple, as I set out for the library.

Chapter 4

Jillian

THE SUMMER HEAT WAS STIFLING. For those wearing cheap rayon blends, it must have been A-OK. But my dry cleaning bill this month was already shaping up to warrant a call from Mommy Dearest. I was already preparing for another fire-breathing tirade from atop her fire-breathing dragon. But it was hopeless. Lowe's office was suffocating.

"So, who's the hobo?" The man in the lobby with the interesting swagger, had been fashion backward in his ill-fitting cargo pants and plain, black T-shirt. He was also desperately in need of a razor, but he smelled like a Christmas tree. The chair I was sitting in smelled like one, too.

"He's not a hobo, Jillian… just a student, same as you." She was *handling* me. Gareth often did that. I hated being handled.

"Really? I didn't realize we allowed bums into our esteemed university now. I worry this may have a negative impact on recruitment if it gets out, but you can trust me. I won't tell." I mimicked the motion of zipping my lips for added effect. She rolled her eyes, clearly immune to my brand of humor.

"Hmm." She mused, tapping her pen on her chin. "I wonder what allowing those with a history of criminal activity would do for recruitment? But don't worry. You can trust me. I won't tell."

Well, okay.

"Now, do you want to tell me why the DA's office called this summer, asking me to help supervise your *community service?*"

"Yeah, about that, I—"

"Jillian, you are a smart girl, but you make some really stupid choices sometimes." *Why was it harder explaining this to my academic advisor than it was telling my own parents?*

"But—" I was ready for my practiced rebuttal, but she stood, sending a piercing glare my way to shut me up. It worked. This woman, all five feet of her, scared me   sometimes.

"I'm not really in the mood for you to make excuses for your behavior or to listen to you whine and blame other people. From what I understand, you got yourself drunk and drove that pretty little sports car of yours into a telephone pole. Does my account of the events sound about right?"

If anyone else had looked at or spoken to me the way this woman did, I'd have their head on a platter.

But Mrs. Lowe had a direct number to my father and, after the summer I'd had, I needed to lay low for a while. "Yes, ma'am, I totaled my car." The look I had plastered on my contrite face wasn't working. Out of practice, I was out of luck.

"And you were hurt, I see?" *Understatement of the year.* I nodded.

I was walking better. I didn't even need a cane for assistance anymore. As long as I took breaks and kept to a slower pace, no one would ever know about my three-month-old injuries.

"Are you feeling better?" Her concern was genuine, but I heard something else in her voice. She held her students to a high standard and I'd disappointed her.

"Yes, I am. Thank you for asking." She nodded, shuffling through files, until she got to mine.

"All right then, Miss Walker, are you ready to declare a major?"

God, I hated this question. I wasn't at college to get anything other than an MRS. degree, and I was well on my way to the ring and the white dress. An actual degree meant nothing to me. There were no degrees in planning charity events or climbing the bejeweled ladder to the Junior League presidency.

"No, I'm not. May I have another semester to figure it out? I promise I'll declare before classes start in the spring." Lie. I'd hopefully be planning my wedding by then.

She took a few deep breaths, thumbing through page after page. I'd only been here a year, why on earth was my record so full?

"This is it, Miss Walker. You'll be finished with your core classes after this semester and you'll *have* to choose a major, got it?" I nodded. "Now, let's discuss this little incident and its subsequent commun—"

"Mrs. Lowe," I interrupted, "I'm sure I don't have to tell you how important it is, this *little incident* staying hush-hush. My father's political career, not to mention my relationship with—"

She held her hand up, halting my words. "You can tell your father, Governor Walker, that his daughter's questionable life choices won't make it back to the fine people of Georgia... nor will it become public knowledge that our own fine governor's son's girlfriend hits the sauce before hopping behind the wheel. But I will tell you this: What you did that night was unacceptable and it was by the grace of God Himself that the only things you killed that night were your ridiculous sports car and an innocent telephone pole."

I couldn't meet her eyes. She was not only disappointed, she was pissed.

"I can only imagine how you wormed your way out of an appropriate consequence, but if the DA expects you to serve our community, then that is exactly what you'll do."

It was like court, all over again, but this time there was no Jamison to defend me. Biting my tongue, I kept reminding myself, this was a means to an end. Get the community service assignment, get it over with, then things will go back to normal. I could do anything for a semester, right?

"Here." She snapped a card down in front of me.

"The Community Cafe? What's this?" The business card had a map on one side and an address on the other.

"The Community Cafe is a student-sponsored, student-run soup kitchen located on the west side of campus."

"Soup kitchen?" This was one of the options the philanthropy committee considered, until we realized we'd probably have to wear hairnets. Anything involving hairnets was an automatic *nope* from me.

"Listen, I don't cook. And I *don't* do food."

Mrs. Lowe sat back in her chair. A knowing, satisfied grin spread across her face as she nodded her head. "You do now."

There had to be a way out of this. I'd call Jamison. My plan had been to play this off as me volunteering *out of the goodness of my heart*, but, being foodservice, my sorority sisters would see right through this.

"The cafe provides free hot meals to anyone in the community on Monday, Wednesday, and Friday of each week. We have no trouble getting volunteers on Monday and Wednesday nights, but Friday is another story. That's where *you* come in."

Visions of beer pong and theme parties with my girls from the Kappa house went up in smoke. Friday night was like the Sabbath in Greek life. Taking away my Friday nights would be the death of what little was left of my social life. After a summer of wheelchairs, walkers, crutches, canes, and physical therapy—my social status was on life support. This would be pulling the plug, for sure.

"Look, Mrs. Lowe, my tax dollars already pay to feed these lazy, jobless degenerates by giving them welfare and food stamps. Why should I have to serve them too? It's degrading." She was ignoring me, something she'd become good at over the last year.

"*Your* tax dollars? From that job you have?" *Ugh.* "I think you'd be surprised at what brings people to the cafe."

I snorted. "Doubt it." I couldn't believe this was happening to me.

"Don't look so sad, Jillian. The good news is, only you and I will know why you're *really* there. You can claim you're volunteering out of the goodness of your big ole squishy heart." She rolled her eyes, thinking, *Yeah, right, like anyone would believe that!* I know this because I had been thinking the exact same thing thirty seconds before. Social suicide, that's what this assignment was.

She handed me some paperwork, already filled out in her neat, unmistakable hand. "Report this Friday for training. You will be expected at five and you should plan to stay until the last person is fed and the last dish is washed. That's usually around nine, give or take."

Well, wasn't this just perfect. I never thought taking one corner a little too tight could ruin my reputation so completely.

After tucking the Community Cafe paperwork into my satchel, I stood. The backs of my legs stuck to the cheap vinyl seat and I inwardly cringed at the idea I'd be wearing the recycled sweat of others for the rest of the day.

The walk to the parking garage in the stifling Texas heat took longer than the drive home. The summer before my freshman year, my father snatched up some land a few blocks from campus and built a row of one and two bedroom condominiums. He let me pick everything from the deep maroon brick on the outside, to the earth tones adorning the walls and countertops inside. I was even given carte blanche when outfitting the one built especially for me.

Each day I passed the majestic condo on the end of

the property, I died a little inside. As part of my penance for the wreck, my father had all of my belongings moved into the smallest unit in the complex. Therefore, my current home had three times the furnishings and decor in only half the space. It was heartbreaking.

The phone was ringing when I unlocked the door and I grabbed it just before the answering machine picked up.

"Hello? I'm here, I'm here." Out of breath was *not* a good sound for me.

"Hey, *hooker*!"

Ugh, Lori. I was too tired to deal with her today. Her voice was like squeaky brakes. And there would never be a moment in time when I wouldn't hear her, and instantly recall the night she had Gareth pressed up against the wall of his fraternity house, mauling his face like a dog with an empty peanut butter jar.

"See Gar," she whined between sloppy licks and kisses. I'd wandered inside the frat house, sick to my stomach from the mountain of vodka-infused jello I'd consumed at the end-of-year luau, when I stumbled upon my best friend and my boyfriend, tucked into the doorway of a locked storage closet. I stopped at the sound of her mewling. "You like me, I know you do." The low rumble of his voice followed, along with more slurping and a little giggle from Lor. I didn't wait around to see where her hand was headed, but as I turned the corner, I heard her whimper "I've got everything she's got. We could be

so good together." I made it to the bathroom just in time to empty the entire contents of my stomach: four red jello shots.

That was the night my life blew up in my face. Literally.

"Yeah, so like, I need your help coming up with a costume for Friday's social at the Kappa House. The theme is 'Barbie Girl in a Barbie World.'" Her Pepto Bismol sing-song voice made me want to hurl.

"At first, I wanted to go as Malibu Barbie, but Janie already called it. I told her you'd probably already claimed that for yourself, so you may need to give her a shout. Anyway, I'm thinking of going as Great Shape Barbie, since I have all that spandex from dance team, but then I thought of Astronaut Barbie. I totally bet I could make that mad slutty." Lori could make a potato sack look slutty, so if that was her goal, it was in the bag.

"What do you think? Which one are you going as?" Janie could be Malibu Barbie for all I cared. No one knew it, but my days of prancing around nearly naked were long over. Now, how to get out of this one...

"Um, so, I have a thing on Friday, actually, so I don't think I'll make it this time." What a total crap situation, since I had the perfect blue lamé jumpsuit and mink stole that would put Janie in her bikini and Lori in her spandex to shame.

"Oh, that's too bad." Could *not* be less genuine if she tried.

"Tell me about it." I was over this convo.

"Hey, it's Kappa's first function of the season. Isn't Gareth coming to town? He *is* the former president."

"Oh, um… I'll call him, but I doubt he can come in from *Harvard* for a little party."

Lori was what my mother referred to as *new money*, an insult of the worst kind. *New money* lacked the sophistication and class of those who'd been born into wealth and privilege. Lori didn't attend cotillion or finishing school. She didn't attend an elite private high school with the children of celebrities and sports greats. She didn't have a full-service, luxury box at Atlanta-Fulton County Stadium, home of the Braves.

No, Lori bought her lipstick and hair dye at the same place she gets her birth control. I only know this because I saw the receipt one time. That was unforgivable in my social circle. She faked it well enough, but Lori is in way over her head buddying up to me. And if she thinks she has a snowball's chance in hell of getting anything other than a drunken make out session from Gareth, she is dumber than she looks.

"Oh. Well, it's probably for the best, anyway."

"Yeah." *Would it be rude to just hang up?*

"Hey, has Angie called you yet?"

"No, Lori, I just got home." I glanced at my answering machine, at the big red digital *three* blinking the same rhythm as my pounding heart. "But I have messages. Why? What does Angie want?"

"Oh, nothing much." Lori's overly cheery tone contradicted her words which were dripping with sugary poison. "*Only* that her maid and Gareth's mother's assistant play bridge together on Monday nights and according to her, Gareth has taken the four-carat diamond ring he inherited from his grandmother to get sized." She ended her revelation on a high note, expecting what, I wasn't sure. My silence upset her. "Hello? Did you hear what I just said?"

I nodded, before realizing she couldn't see me. "Yes, yes, I heard you." It was like my breath was stolen right out of my chest. "But, she must be mistaken. Isn't this a little soon?" But was it really? Hadn't I just been hoping for this moment so I could ditch college and live the life I was meant to lead?

"Too soon? Are you high? Gareth Baines Johnson, son of Texas governor Thomas Mitchell Johnson, grandson of the late president of the United-"

"Lori, stop, Jesus." I couldn't think. My head felt like someone set fire to a fireworks stand. "Tone down the drama a few decibels. I'm well-aware of my boyfriend's genealogy." My heart was using my stomach as a trampoline and despite having skipped lunch, I felt vomit creeping up into my throat. *What's wrong with me?*

"Then what's this talk about '*too soon*?' I mean, you *are* dating the most eligible bachelor in the state and I just told you there is a good chance he's planning to propose soon. This is what you've been dreaming about, right? Aren't you the least bit excited?"

Of course I was excited, right? "Of course I'm excited. God, Lori, you just took me off guard. And of course I was expecting something like this eventually, but not quite this soon. Did she mention a timeline?"

"Well, actually she did. Clear your calendar for Christmas break, sweetie, because I have it on good authority you're being whisked away to Aspen! I wonder if there's a Snowbunny Barbie? That would be totally cute."

Chapter 5

Bennett

THE SIX STORY LIBRARY, built in the seventies from sand-toned brick, sat right in the middle of campus and the doors opened at six in the morning. It smelled of old books, stale coffee, and freshly sharpened pencils. I'd spent many an hour scoping out the routines of the people who ran the place and it was a rare day when an employee arrived any earlier than 5:45. And even then, the library aides, most of them student workers, didn't make their way up to the stacks until much later.

My military alarm clock woke me at five o'clock on the dot, which fit my new arrangement perfectly. Leaving the fifth floor bathroom in the east wing of the library with a good fifteen minutes to spare, I stopped short when I turned a corner and ran right into a giant wall of a man.

My towel, around my shoulders just seconds before, had fallen across the toes of the man's brown leather boots, leaving me completely bare from the waist up, water still dripping from my beard.

"Ahh, man, it's not… " Then I stopped, squared my shoulders, and looked him in the eyes. I was six feet tall, but this guy was at least two heads taller. His bulky arms folded over his chest like a club bouncer and could barely cover it. Dressed in what looked to be an official university polo and pressed khaki pants, I wondered if he might be security, but I hoped to hell he wasn't. I'd seen him around. He was hard to miss, the man was a brick wall. Impenetrable. "Well, sir, I'm not gonna lie. This is exactly what it looks like."

I could hear the theme song from "The Good, the Bad, and the Ugly" playing in my head and it took everything in me to keep from cracking a smile at the absurdity of the whole thing. After a few long minutes, the brick wall spoke.

"Follow me." Two words and he turned and walked toward the stairwell, confident I would do as he commanded. I'd planned to at least stop and grab my rucksack, but as we neared the door to the stairs, I saw it was already waiting for me there. So I swung it over my shoulder and followed the man to meet my fate. I knew I was in the clear when he started whistling the theme song from "The Good, the Bad, and the Ugly."

For a large man, he was agile. Sure, four flights of stairs were nothing, going down, but for a man his size, I expected him to be more out of breath. When we reached the bottom floor, I expected to take the double doors into the main part of the library. That would place us a few feet away from the large circulation desk, where 'the wall' would then call campus police and I'd either be ticketed or just thrown out. *Campus police didn't have lockup, did they?*

But instead of leading me out into the library, we turned the opposite direction, ducking through a small, nondescript door I hadn't ever noticed before. The space was stupid small, but it didn't help that 'the wall' stood right in the center.

"That right there makes out into a bed." He started barking information about what appeared to be a small apartment. "Through that door, you'll find a toilet, shower, and an ancient, stackable washer and dryer. They worked, last I checked, but I've never been able to figure out what those were ever used for here." I wondered how he knew they worked, but he didn't seem the type to answer questions. It was strange, really. I was trained to read people, anticipate their every move, but *this* I did *not* see coming.

He took my bag from me, placing it in a floor-to-ceiling cabinet. "This here's your closet and your pantry." That's when I noticed a microwave sitting on a shelf within the closet.

"Food service stores the vending machine snacks that have almost expired in here. Help yourself, though I'd steer clear of the cherry pies unless you've got good dental coverage. That's one snack that probably actually expires *before* the date on the package." He chuckled at his own joke while I looked around for Dick Clark and the *Candid Camera* crew. That show was still on, right?

"Sir, just curious, but why did you bring me here?" Valid question, though it could have been executed in a more masculine way. I was starting to get antsy, both from being in such a small space with 'The Hulk,' *and* because I was slowly realizing all the combat training in the world couldn't have prepared me to take this guy on in the event his switch flipped.

"This used to be the employee break room, but when we remodeled a few years ago we built a bigger one, so this room just sits here." Oh. Well. That answers… nothing.

"I don't—"

He chuckled again.

"Sorry, just realized you have no idea who I am. I'm Lillie Lowe's husband." His bright, toothy grin completely transformed his imposing character into someone I'd sit and watch a game with over a beer.

"Oh, wow, it's nice to meet you." And since his introduction calmed the ninjas kicking and chopping my insides, I offered my hand. "Your wife is a miracle worker. She saved my ass this semester!"

The low timbre of his voice made his laugh smooth and rich, reminding me of a chocolate waterfall. "She had me keep an eye out for you. She was afraid you didn't have a place to live."

I ducked my head as heat spread up my neck and over my cheeks. Knowing I was homeless, stowing away in the nooks and crannies of the library, was one thing. But having to admit it to a perfect, albeit well-meaning, stranger brought me to a whole new level of pathetic.

"Truth is, sir, I'd have reenlisted if for nothing more than three square meals a day and a roof over my head, but that wasn't an option." I could have gone further, told him the whole truth, but my story was just that. Mine. And it was really all I had.

"You know, pride can be a pretty strong barrier between two people, son. If you'll swallow a little of that and let us help you, I think your situation will start to improve." The man spoke from the heart and oddly, I felt like he shrank in size. He wasn't intimidating anymore. He was one of the good guys. Maybe he was the exact friend I needed.

He crossed the room, running a finger over the surfaces, checking for dust. There was none. "We all hit rough patches and I don't know what you've gone through to land you here today, but see this as a second chance." I knew every word he spoke was true and came from a good place, but it didn't make accepting charity any easier.

"Well, Mr. Lowe," I tipped my head up to meet his kind eyes. "I thank you for all of this, but I won't take advantage. I'll figure something out soon."

He was already shuffling out of the room, waving away my words. "No worries on my end. You clearly know how this building works, so just stay invisible, keep doing what you're doing, and you'll be fine. But it does look like you could use some meat on those bones of yours. I left some information on the counter about a free meal program we have on campus. It's a good distance from here, but it's worth it, I promise!"

"Thank you, Mr. Lowe." I called after him.

"Mr. Lowe is my father. Please, just call me Chance."

Chapter 6

Jillian

"HELLO?" I knocked on the front doors of the Community Cafe once again, but after standing in the ninety-eight degree heat in jeans and a cute cropped school tee, I was starting to get annoyed. No answer, and looking through the tinted glass doors would have required pushing my face up against it, so *that* wasn't happening. After a few more minutes, I walked around the building, looking for signs of life.

The oven-hot air in back stank of cooked garbage and week-old milk. A perfect recipe for nausea. The heavy metal door sat slightly ajar, so after a few deep breaths through my mouth, I ventured in. "Hello, I'm here to volunteer?"

I knew I was in the right place the moment I opened the door. Sparkling white tile gleamed, reflecting the sun, and the aroma of fresh cooked meat made me wish I'd had more than a SlimFast for lunch. My stomach growled in agreement. I took a tentative step inside, but given the clientele, I was hesitant to walk further and catch someone off guard. I didn't think I could handle being stabbed and mugged by some vagrant, along with everything else I was currently dealing with.

"Come on back, I'm in the kitchen!" The male voice was pleasant enough, but turning the corner, I collided with a mountain of a man. He towered over me at 7 feet tall and wore a Cheshire cat grin. He obviously spent *a lot* of time in the gym. His arms were massive and his rippling skin was black as night, all the way up to his shiny bald head. I saw the giant knife in his hand and suddenly every gory Freddy Krueger movie that terrified me as a child flashed before my eyes. Oh crap! *Now what?* I felt like running for the hills.

"Jillian?" I about came out of my boots at Mrs. Lowe's voice suddenly materializing behind me. All the air I hadn't realized I was holding in my lungs whooshed out in one long breath and my legs almost liquefied. She was sneaky, that one.

"This is my husband, Chance." She turned her attention to the man, who was now running a towel up and down the large knife. "Chance, this is Jillian Walker. She'll be volunteering with us here on Friday nights for… a while." I exhaled. Man, was I glad I hadn't run. That would have been hard to explain.

"Mr. Lowe, nice to meet you." I craned my head and found myself staring into two gleaming eyes peering down at me. I felt like a field mouse under the gaze of a hawk. By reflex I stuck out my hand, just like my father taught me.

But mid-reach I changed my mind. His hands were covered in bright yellow gloves that were slick with a substance I didn't want to think about. I deflected my hand and swept a loose strand of hair out of my eyes instead. Better safe than sorry until I learned the proper protocol for greeting new help. I needed to get up to speed… we'd had the same woman working in our kitchen since before I was born.

The state-of-the-art kitchen was a dream, but looked like it belonged in an stately home, rather than this sad little soup kitchen. And it was *enormous*. I couldn't help thinking how all these lovely amenities were being wasted on those too lazy to work. However, a delicious aroma hung in the air like a mist. There were pots bubbling, something baking, and a freshly cut salad in huge, clear plastic tubs covered in Saran wrap. Mr. Lowe stirred something in a metal pot, then slid the two salad tubs into the massive refrigerator, one-handed and with ease.

"Chance has everything just about ready, but you can go put your purse in the office, right there," she gestured toward a little room off to the left with her hand, "then put on one of the aprons in there and meet me in the dining room. It's that way." She headed in the opposite direction and I went in search of an apron, knowing it would be nothing like the one I'd donned last Halloween for my 'oh, so scandalous' French maid costume.

The dining area was spacious and looked exactly like this mom-and-pop diner back home called Pig's Feet. It was a place my mother wouldn't be caught dead in, but they had incredible meat pies and sometimes our housekeeper would sneak me one.

The floor was maroon and white checkered tile, just as clean and beautiful as the kitchen, and the walls were covered in what appeared to be old fence boards. The tables were all shapes, sizes, and colors—and not one chair matched another—but the chaos of it all only added to the charm and appeal of the place.

Preparing for the dinner rush was my assigned duty. Mr. Lowe stayed in the kitchen, while his wife and I rolled silverware, filled ice machines, brought out package after package of plastic cups and Styrofoam plates, and even brewed my very first batch of tea in a four-gallon, stainless steel dispenser. After filling more salt and peppershakers than seemed necessary for a week, much less one evening meal, Mrs. Lowe opened the doors and started inviting the poor people in.

For the first several minutes, I stood next to Mrs. Lowe like a lemming and watched as she smiled and shook hands with a variety of people. The group—old and young, black and white—was as eclectic as the furniture they'd be eating on.

"What do I do now?" I whispered. I'd donned my newly claimed neon green apron with the turquoise pocket and tied my hair up in the most severe bun I could handle, as to avoid the dreaded hairnet. I was there, I was cute, and I was ready to get the night over with.

"Today, just watch how we do things. Next week, expect to play a much larger role." I stood off to the side and watched Lillie Lowe behave as if she were hosting a state dinner, as I busied my mind with what circumstances brought all these people to the cafe. It was interesting, really, how she seemed to know everyone's name, even the children. And boy, were there *a lot* of children. Chance knew them all too, and they made small talk as they worked their way toward the buffet-style serving line.

The chalkboard menu, in large loopy letters, boasted the day's fare: barbecued chicken, green beans, mashed potatoes with gravy, and a green salad. The food appeared like magic, in big troughs. Chance made quick work of stocking the heated buffet table, and once the line got going it was all hands on deck.

"Jill?" Chance was hollering over his shoulder as he scraped the last of the gravy from a large, cylindrical bucket-type container.

"It's Jillian, please. Call me Jillian." I harbored a deep hatred for the name Jill, way down in my gut, and I always would.

"My apologies, Miss Jillian. Could you be a dear and take this back to the sink? If you're feeling especially energetic, you could run some hot water into it. It'll sure make it easier for you to clean later."

Easier for *me* to clean? My first inclination was to snap back with a snide comment about him washing his own damn giant gravy bucket. But I bit back the words, hid my disgust with a smile, and did what Chance Lowe asked of me.

When I returned, he was laughing at something a young boy was saying. When the child joined his family at one of the tables, I was taught where to find the replacement tubs of food in an upright warming oven right by the kitchen door. "When I call out a food, it means I'm running low. Go grab a replacement, we can switch the empty one for the full, and we'll never even miss a beat." That was the most I'd heard him say all night.

Chance's accent was as smooth as the whipped butter I'd set out to pair with the fresh baked rolls, but its origin was unmistakable. "Are you from New Orleans, Mr. Lowe?"

A chuckle rolled from his throat like thunder announcing a summer storm. "Naw, hon… just outside though. Is it that obvious?" I nodded and, for the first time in ages, I smiled and it wrinkled my eyes.

"Miss Jillian!" I was being summoned to the buffet line from my place, where I was restocking napkins, straws, and cup lids. "Grab you a plate, honey.

Looks like we're gonna have a lot leftover."

I glanced into the stainless steel containers, each still at least half-full of the Southern food that must have taken hours to prepare, and shook my head.

"No thank you, Mr., uhh, Chance. I think I'll pass tonight." The wrinkles on his forehead said he took my rejection personally. I turned back to my task, pretending I hadn't noticed.

"Hey Chance, I'll take some. It smells so good I think I gained three pounds just sniffing the air on the way in here."

I was too poised to whip around and get a look at who that voice belonged to, so I let my mind imagine someone big, strong. A cop maybe, based on the authoritative tone. It was deep, masculine. It was something I wanted to hear again. But, it also belonged to a poor person. And I belonged to Gareth.

"Bennett, so glad you could make it! Help yourself."

From the corner of my eye, I saw Chance step aside, allowing the man access to the heated table. And only after he'd found a seat and Mrs. Lowe had sat down beside him, did I allow my eyes to drink him in. I recognized him as the man who was leaving her office just as I was entering a few days before.

"Um, Chance?" I'd moved to the serving side of the table where the man was starting to disassemble things, and spoke under my breath. "Who is that man Mrs. Lowe is sitting with?"

"Oh, that's Bennett."

"And, he's a student?" Chance nodded, continuing to wipe things down. He motioned for me to consolidate the half-empty food containers, but I kept my eye on the man and Mrs. Lowe, noticing their relaxed demeanor and easy banter. I was envious. I don't think I'd ever been that comfortable with anyone in my life.

As tacky as they were, I'd never been so grateful for Styrofoam plates and plastic cutlery in my life. Washing just the dishes used to cook and serve took longer than the cafe was even open for business. "Don't you have any other employees, besides you and Mrs. Lowe?" It was barbaric for anyone to assume two people could manage this on their own, even with a volunteer here and there. I threw my apron into a bin to be washed, Chance handed me my purse, and we made our way back to the dining room and to the front doors.

"No, ma'am. This is a non-profit organization. Lillie and I started this cafe after our son did a project in school about homeless shelters and the lack of hot food. This is something we did as a family." Where was their son, then? Shouldn't he at least be here helping? Opening the door, he ushered me out in front of him.

"So, you aren't paid to be here? I mean, why? Why would anyone work this hard for nothing?" He locked the door behind him, slipping the key into his pocket.

"You know, at first, we did it for our son, to show him the value of giving back to a community that had given so much to him. But, now he's gone, so I guess we do it in his memory." We'd been walking, but stopped when we reached an old beater pickup truck.

"So, you lost your son?" Mrs. Lowe had been my academic advisor for over a year, but I didn't know her. I hadn't met her husband until tonight and I had no idea she even had a son. Maybe that says something about me.

"Yeah, he died in Kuwait, about eighteen months ago." My heart squeezed and the automatic words of sympathy caught in my throat.

I will never forget the sound coming from my throat the day I got the news my best friend had been killed. I will never forget the heart-seizing, gut-wrenching pain that came with the knowledge we'd never sneak off to the creek together, or fly halfway across the river on the rope swing before falling in. I will never forget losing the one person in the world I could actually be myself around without the fear of judgment.

"My best friend died over there."

He nodded, placing his hand on my shoulder. That was the first time I'd said it aloud and the first time anyone had shown me sympathy for my loss. I worried I may let my mask slip, which wouldn't be acceptable behavior for a woman of my station.

"Well, anyway," I waved away any hint of emotion that might seep out and slipped right back into the role of my mother's daughter. "I can understand keeping the cafe running in memory of your son, but I'm concerned all these lazy vagrants, dirty drifters, and good-for-nothing bums are taking advantage of your kindness." Chance smiled as he folded himself into the small truck cab.

"It's not my job to find out what brought them to my door. Everyone carries their own burdens. I'm only here to put food in their bellies and hopefully a smile on their faces a few nights a week. The rest of it is between them and God." He started his engine as he tapped the horn to get his wife's attention. She'd been talking to one of the poor people, the man with the sexy voice, I think. She waved goodbye, hurried into the passenger seat, and they drove off into the night.

It didn't take but a glance at my car to see something was off. "Damn it!" I marched over, kneeling down to see the shiny nail stuck into my deflated driver's side tire. This day could go to hell.

"Can I help you out with that?" My heart about jumped out of my throat as I looked up into the face of the man Chance called Bennett. Yep, he was every bit as delicious as his voice indicated, with cheekbones sharp as a machete and closely cropped hair the exact color of a Hershey's bar. Standing, I brushed my hands off on my jeans.

"No, don't worry. I have a car phone for just such an emergency. I can call the dealership. They have roadside assistance."

He laughed. "Yeah, I'm sure they do, at 9:00 on a Friday night. Give me the keys." He held his hand out.

"What? No, I'm not giving you the keys to my brand-new Beamer. You're nuts." *Sure, poor, possibly homeless man... I'll just hand over my keys so you can stab me with a shank, stuff me in the trunk, and ride off into the sunset in my $40,000 vehicle, paper plates from the dealer still attached.* He wasn't going to charm me with that hunky, husky voice of his.

"Nuts? Maybe... but right now I'm all you got, so pop that trunk?"

"Excuse me? What the hell do you need out of my trunk?" My voice was at least two octaves higher than usual and I prayed the Lowes lived the rest of their lives with the guilt of knowing they left me all alone with this murderer with the bronze-colored eyes and smooth as silk voice.

"Well, I'd like to get your spare out and change this tire before we both melt. Just because the sun's gone down doesn't mean the temperature has."

He leaned into the trunk to retrieve the spare and whatever else he needed to fix the flat, and in doing that, flexed some muscles that made my temperature rise. I physically fanned my heated cheeks, shaking my head. No, I could *not* be looking at this guy's perfectly sculpted ass and massive thighs. I was spoken for. And no matter how many times I said that to myself, I only looked away a split second before he turned back around. And oh, those arms.

"Can I, I dunno, hold the flashlight for you at least?" He grunted and shook his head, already jacking up the car. So I grabbed my car phone, stood back, and let him get to it so I could get home.

I called home to check my answering machine. After leaving several messages on Gareth's machine, it was about damn time for him to return one of my calls.

"Hey, babe, sorry I've been MIA lately, this semester is already kicking my ass. I'm calling to see if you have plans over Christmas break—I was thinking we could go up to the Aspen cottage. Let me know. Bye."

Finally, there it was. Aspen. Just as Lori predicted. Three months ago—even three weeks ago—all I wanted was this: an invite to a posh ski resort, a diamond ring, and a question I'd been promised since I first had hormones. Yet, all I could focus on was the sight in front of me.

Homeless or not, the man made changing a tire look like a well-rehearsed dance, with the heavy steel light perched efficiently between his shoulder and his head like a telephone receiver. It was impossible not to notice how his grey T-shirt, with ARMY printed across his chest in block letters, started to dampen as it stretched across his broad, muscular shoulders.

I meandered closer and got a whiff of his clean, sweaty, manly smell. I leaned in for more while he made the dirty work of loosening, screwing, and fastening look like child's play and in just a few more minutes, I was afraid I'd once again be roadworthy.

"You're good at that." I'd be lying if I said I wasn't disappointed the shirt hadn't come off. It was wicked hot.

"Yeah, well. When the *difference* of a few minutes could mean the *difference* between life and death, you learn to be quick." I was all for dramatics, but something told me he wasn't exaggerating, which made me even more curious as to who this dark-haired stranger really was. I sat on the curb.

"Stop biting." I yanked my finger from my mouth and narrowed my eyes at Bennett as he tightened a lug nut on my spare.

"I wasn't biting—," I spat, the lie coming to my lips as naturally as breathing. He reminded me of my brother, with the nagging.

"Oh yeah, tell that to your cuticles." With a grunt, he grabbed the deflated tire and popped it back in the trunk, followed by the lug wrench and the jack. "All right, you're good to go."

"Thank you. I'm Jillian, by the way." I extended my arm, but was grateful when he backed away, showing me his blackened palms.

"Bennett Hanson and you're welcome. It's nice to meet you, Jill."

"Don't call me Jill. My name is Jillian." My mother always said, upper-crust, well-bred girls did not tolerate nicknames.

"Oh. Sorry."

"Look, can I pay you or something?" I ducked inside for my wallet, but he was already several feet from the car.

"No, thank you." He kept walking to the spigot on the side of the building to wash his hands. I looked up and down the street for signs of Bennett Hanson's truck, but came up empty. We were in College Station, where the pickup truck to good ole boy ratio was high, so it was easy to assume that was this man's chosen mode of transportation.

"Can I at least give you a ride to your car?" The question surprised me as much as it did him. He stopped and turned, cocking his head to one side.

"No, I can manage. I certainly wouldn't want to *take*

advantage of your kindness." And turning on his toes, he started toward campus with a smile on his face and a bounce in his step.

I watched Bennett walk toward campus, backpack slung over his right shoulder, left hand in his pocket. When he turned a corner and was out of sight, I pulled out and headed down Jersey toward home.

Who was Bennett Hanson? And why was he at a soup kitchen? Clearly, that hadn't been his first visit. He and Chance had a special rapport and his bond with Mrs. Lowe was touching. She looked at him the way I imagine she most likely looked at her son when he was still alive. My heart hiccuped as memories tried to surface, but I pushed them back down. I was taught to bury my feelings, never show emotion.

The whole ride home, my mind was consumed with one man, and it wasn't the one who was having a four-carat diamond ring fitted to my finger.

Chapter 7

Bennett

"Chance, get off man!" I gasped, using all my strength to pull much needed oxygen into my lungs. Between the weight of his body and the raw heat, I was suffocating, each breath dragging more and more fine desert sand into my lungs. I coughed, sputtering as I tried to draw a deep breath. "Chance! Move!"

"No, man! If I move, you die!" We were in the bunks at basic training, worlds away from any real dangers. But the unmistakable rattle of gunfire echoed through the night and the shouts of soldiers just outside were nothing short of frantic.

"Dude, this isn't funny. Off. Now." As I tried to push him off, he laughed. What started low and rough, morphed into something loud and full, coming from somewhere deep inside my friend. It was unlike anything I'd ever heard come from Chance's mouth.

He rolled off, clutching the battle worn picture in his bloody hand over his heart. "I forgot to save the arms, man, I'm sorry. I forgot all about the arms." Sure enough, what I'd been using to push him off were gone, now only bloody stumps at the elbows.

"They don't hurt." I raised them, inspecting the beauty of the red muscle against bright white bone, jagged at the break. "Why don't they hurt?" I look over and see Chance has my hands in his, dangling them over where I lay.

"They can't hurt, Ben. They're gone. I didn't save them. Remember?" He was monotone, looking at the bloody scrap of a picture on the ground at his feet. "Ben, you don't have arms. Now you can't hold her. You can't hold my golden girl. You don't have arms, but don't worry Ben. I can hold her with your arms.

He then began trying to grab the picture using my hands like the claw machine you'd see at an arcade.

I sat straight up, letting the darkness of the room wrap around me like a warm blanket on a winter morning. My arms, curled tight around my midsection, had fallen asleep. As I bent and moved each finger, pins and needles took over, reminding me they were still very much attached.

What the hell was that about? I shook my head, trying to shake off the residue of the dream. His golden girl. I didn't even know her name. All I know is he grew up in New York. In the Bronx, actually. He was all The Yankees are bad asses, they're gonna kick the Astro's farmer asses this year. Truth? I didn't care, but when he started talking smack about Houston, I became the 'Stro's biggest fan. It was a guy thing, something I hadn't known much about before joining the army and meeting Chance.

It had crossed my mind more than once that I should try to find his golden girl. Did she know he was dead? Did she even exist? And how on earth would I find her with no name, a picture almost worn clean of ink, and the name of a soldier who let her live in his heart?

I'd spent more time than I'd like to admit watching the sun push the darkness away, craving that same relief. It was nights like this I wish I'd never surrendered to sleep. Pulling out the picture from my wallet, I looked again, willing something to pop out at me. A pudgy face with braces and what appeared to be dark hair, dark eyes. I just described more than half the population of Brooklyn.

Trudging out of bed, I started a pot of coffee before heading toward the shower. Fridays were always tough, thanks to 8:00 a.m. statistics. It wouldn't have been my first choice, but beggars can most certainly not be choosers. I was lucky to be enrolled at all. Plus, math and I got along just fine, so this was a fluff class for me.

The water took a millennium to heat up, but this was an odd morning. I actually had time to wait. I was caught up on homework and reading, and the night I changed Jill's—no, Jillian's tire—I'd come right back and used a computer on the third floor to knock out the paper I'd been writing for my sociology class.

When steam started escaping from under the

bathroom door, I jumped in and stood completely still, letting the water run over my tired body. Hot showers were another thing falling under the 'You don't know what you've got 'til it's gone' category. There are so many things in life I'd taken for granted that the army taught me to appreciate. Hot showers, real food, beautiful women.

And there she was, in my mind, just like she was that night. Any red-blooded man would have appreciated watching her bend and stretch as she replenished the supplies, but when Jillian turned around, all coherent thought left my brain. I'd been speaking with Mrs. Lowe and there's no way she missed how my words evaporated into thin air and how my eyes affixed to Jillian, following her for the rest of the night.

The pull of gravity was stronger in Texas than it was overseas. It probably had something to do with the twenty-four/ seven adrenaline high of combat. Seeing Jillian that night brought that high right back. That apron tied around her slim waist created an off-key harmony with the stylish, name brand clothing hugging her curves, but it also served as a mask. I saw through her artifice though. I saw her. In the moments when she spoke with Chance, she let her guard down and her true self emerged. That girl, the one humming George Strait as she washed dishes, wiggling her hips to the beat when she thought no one was watching. That girl was someone the old Bennett Hanson would have given a limb to love.

Dressed and ready for class a full hour earlier than planned, I crept into Chance's office, grabbed the phone receiver, and started dialing. The call was well overdue.

"Hello?" Her tone held a tremor I'd equate to fear. God, it was good to hear her voice.

"Rosie!" I heard the rustle of her covering the phone while she barked admonitions to whoever was in her kitchen. I imagine it was something like, Settle down and zip it, I'm on the phone. I have a wooden spoon and I'm not afraid to use it, or something like that.

"Mijo?" My son? I laughed.

"Yeah, one of them. Now you get to figure out which." Rosie and Doc had fostered nearly a hundred kids over the years on their ranch. Well, technically, now it was my ranch too, but it would always be their ranch.

"Bravo, you think I do not know you when you call me? But I shouldn't, should I? I should forget your voice, you call me so little, but I will always know mi bravo." Bravo. Brave. She'd called me that since I stepped on her porch as a skinny, know-it-all who had no use for a short, squatty Mexican woman who tried to wipe my face with her dish towel before she even introduced herself.

"I sure do miss you, old woman." I could hear her smile over the phone and I felt it in my gut. It may have never been official, but this was my family and I think I missed them now more than I had when I was more than seven thousand miles away.

"How is class? Are you paying attention? Keeping up with your studies? You're a smart boy, Bravo. Very smart."

"It's good, Rosie. I have a little apartment. And I have a job working in the library." It was true. Due to my financial aid paperwork, essentially stating I had zero dollars, Chance was able to hire me as a student worker. I worked when I could, after hours, copying old documents in sets to be sent to different campus libraries within the Texas A&M University system. I can't say it's the most stimulating work, but I essentially get paid to push a few buttons and study, so no complaints here.

"What's wrong?"

"Nothing. Why would you think something's wrong?" I swear she was involved in some Mexican voodoo. She knew what was up from hundreds of miles away.

"No me mientas."

"I'm not lying. I'm just not sleeping."

"Pesadillas?" Nightmares? She whispered it like a revelation, not a question.

"Yeah. It's getting better though. It's not as bad as it was."

"Como se llama?"

"Rosie. Sweetie. I don't speak Spanish. But who? I haven't met anyone special."

"Mentira." She mumbled under her breath.

"Her name is Jillian. I changed her tire. She's highborn, you can tell, and she'd never give a second look to a guy like me." I sighed. "Besides, I'm not here to find a girl. That's the last thing I want to do."

"Bonita?" Grrr. She never listened. I dropped my chin to my chest, mourning once again the man I was and the man I could have been.

"Muy bonita." And she was. She will make some man terribly happy. Hell, she might be with him right now, waking up in his bed, stretching out like a cat, before flopping back down for a few more minutes of sleep in his arms, lucky bastard.

"Come home, Mijo."

"I can't. I have to work. I have class. I'm taking a full load and if I don't stay on top of it, I'll drown." But I wanted to. I really wanted to. I could work on the ranch without thought. Doc and I could work side by side for ten hours and exchange even fewer words. It was familiar. It was safe. But being on the ranch wasn't moving me forward in life.

"Te amo mi cielo." Oh, she was laying it on thick.

"I'll try and come home for Christmas, Mama."

"I'll send you a bus ticket. And Benito? You are a good boy and you are so easy to love. Don't ever forget."

I hung up the phone, lonelier than I'd been before. I'd always been part of something bigger. I entered the system at fifteen after both of my parents were imprisoned for running a drug ring out of our shanty in East Texas. From there, I was sent to a foster ranch, where I met Rosie and Doc. For the next three years, they did their best to infuse into me all the love I'd missed out on in a household where I remained invisible… albeit tough to do most of the time.

The day I turned eighteen, I enlisted in the US Army and the rest is history. Now, four years later, I'm stronger, smarter, and despite my current living situation, I feel more stable than I have in years. But I'd be lying if I said I didn't miss being part of a group. I thought all this alone time was what I needed, if for nothing else than to sort myself out and get my mind right. But the persistent silence was doing more harm than good.

All day long, I'd been debating dinner. I was surviving fine on bread, peanut butter, and whatever else I could pick up at the general store on the edge of campus for weeks, but the idea of a hot meal was too much to resist.

I hadn't returned to The Community Cafe for

their infamous big Friday night dinner since I'd changed Princess Jillian's tire a few weeks before. The Monday/ Wednesday dinners were different. Sometimes breakfast food, once a big salad bar, and a few days before, when the temperature dropped, they served soup and sandwiches. I enjoyed those meals, but I'd been dreaming of all-American beef for a month. I think part of me still struggled with the whole charity aspect of things, but another part of me knew Friday was the day she was there. I had no desire to see the mix of pity and disgust in Jillian's eyes when she looked at me in that place. I could go a lifetime without hot food to spare myself from that look again.

"Hey, wait! Bennett?" I was thinking of food, deciding if I should shower or not, as I entered the library. But hearing my name, I stopped cold. I'd gotten so good at skirting past the circulation desk undetected, but it was Friday afternoon—the place was deader than disco, and I feared my cover had been blown.

It was cool, I was cool. I certainly wasn't a stowaway in the weird little hobbit hole under the stairs this guy may or may not even know about.

"Yes?" Oh, it was the guy I'd named Napoleon. Hardly taller than the desk itself, but built like a brick outhouse to compensate for his 'shortcomings' I guessed. I must have smiled at the thought because the guy's face broke out in a wide grin.

"Hey, glad I caught you. Chance wanted me to

give this to you." He held out a book, wrapped in a nondescript plastic sack. "He said you might come through, so I've been looking for you." Great, Chance. Way to keep this thing on the down low.

"He's usually here at this time, right?" I asked, wondering why he hadn't just given it to me himself.

"Well, yeah, but it's barbecue day at the cafe, so he had to go tend to the smokers or pull the pork or some other nonsense."

"Okay. Well, thanks—" I waited, wishing I was less of an introvert at times like these.

"Oh, Leon." He smiled and pointed to his ID tag. "My name is Leon."

And I know I laughed at that. I certainly wouldn't ever forget NapoLEON's name." I waved and we turned in opposite directions, him going back to his job and me going to, what, my apartment? Sure, that worked for the time being.

Once safely inside the confines of my temporary dwelling, I removed the book from the bag. Only it wasn't a book, it was two freakishly thick magazines. The first, The New England Journal of Medicine, dated a few weeks back and the second, Psychology Today, was more recent. Both, I noticed, had pages flagged, but there was also an envelope tucked behind the cover of one.

Bennett,

Today is barbecue day at the cafe and I sure hope you'll join us. Lillie says you're losing weight and I only seem to pass you on your way out. I can always drop a plate by, but it wouldn't kill you to get out and socialize a bit.

So, because it's barbecue day, I had to leave early, which means I had to come in early. That being said, I heard you having a hard time in there this morning. Dreams, I'm guessing?

I don't mean to pry, but my father had CSR (Combat Stress Reaction) after coming home from fighting on the Pacific front in WWII. There wasn't much known about it back then, but in the last ten years, that's changed. I marked some articles that might put words to what you're going through and, when you're ready, I'd like to point you in the right direction to get some help.

Hope to see you tonight,

Chance

Chapter 8

Jillian

"LORI… I HAVE, LIKE, FIVE minutes and then I have to report for duty." It was barbecue day, which only happened once a month, and proved to be the busiest. It seemed as though the entire impoverished population of College Station could smell the smoker and came running. I guess I couldn't blame them. Chance was a magician in the kitchen.

My stomach had been doing funny things at the mere thought of tonight. The last barbecue day, my first time volunteering at The Community Cafe, was also the night I met Bennett Hanson. Or as I like to refer to him, Mr. Distraction. Because that's exactly what he was.

"Jillian, are you even listening to me? God, what has gotten into you? Are you sure you didn't hit your head in that wreck?"

Why was this girl my friend again? Oh right, politics. Her step-grandfather, which she acquired with her mother's third husband and a couple million dollars a few years back, was waiting in the wings for some old geezer on the Supreme Court to die, and my father thought that connection would be beneficial. I was taught at an early age not to befriend anyone unless they had something to offer.

"I'm sorry, Lor, what were you saying?" I checked my makeup in the visor mirror, then checked the time. 4:52. Wow. I was early. That was a first.

"I was saying that Daddy Ron said we could go anywhere I wanted for Christmas break, so I thought about Aspen! Wouldn't that be so awesome, celebrating your *engagement?* On the slopes? Together?"

Of course she *would* choose Aspen. As I opened my mouth to give an opinion I hadn't yet formed, Mrs. Lowe pulled up next to me and waved. "Um, Lori, I have to scoot, it's time for my meeting, but that is a very interesting idea and I will give it some thought." *Not.* I hung up the phone and zipped it up in its black leather pouch, before tucking it under the seat.

Even as recently as a few months ago, the idea of celebrating my engagement to a man as rich and powerful as Gareth Johnson was all-consuming, every moment filled with planning and plotting to fulfill my destiny. But for some reason, these days it was having the opposite effect.

In fact, I found myself seeking out distractions to avoid thinking about it. I should have poured myself into my studies, or my sorority, but those things meant so little these days. In most cases, the distraction had a scruffy, auburn beard, piercing tan eyes, and lips the color of summer raspberries.

I shook all thoughts of Bennett Hanson away and trudged up to the back door of the cafe, refusing to be even one minute early on principle.

Things were relatively quiet and if I hadn't smelled the barbecue, I may have questioned if I'd gotten my days mixed up. "Hello?" I called, but I was greeted by silence. I placed my purse in the office, but when I turned to grab my apron from the hook, it was gone.

"Where's my apron?" Sure, there were other aprons, but I wanted *my apron*. I'd stocked the pockets with paper napkins and plastic utensils, anything to avoid having to run all over the place during the rush.

Water started running in the kitchen about that time, echoing down the hall. Peeking around the corner, I spotted Chance at the sink. Back home, I was famous for my temper. I learned from a young age, the louder I screamed, the more likely I was to get my way. But with the water on full blast, no one would be able to hear me no matter how big a fit I threw, so I stomped down the hall and right up to Chance. Tapping him on the shoulder, I squared my own. "Where is my apron?"

"Oh, is this the apron you're screeching about?" Sure enough, strolling in from the dining room was none other than Bennett Hanson, wearing *my* apron.

"So you say this is yours? I wasn't aware we had assigned aprons."

A slight, indecipherable smirk crept to his lips as he drank me in, head to toe. Had he been anyone else, he'd be walking away with my handprint across his face, but there was something about his eyes that spoke to me. They held an intensity I'd never been witness to before, almost like his gaze had hands, touching me in all the right places. I caught Chance's eye. He was enjoying the show.

"Why are you even wearing an apron? Those are for the volunteers." Hands on hips, I'm sure I more resembled a defiant toddler than a grown woman.

"Well, it seems as though you just answered your own question." He started toward me, slowly untying the knot at his back. "But, please, please… " He lifted the apron off over his head and presented it to me with a flourish. "I beg of you, Princess Jillian, forgive me for my transgression. I vow to never, *ever* don your green and turquoise apron again." *Princess Jillian?*

Rolling my eyes, I snatched the apron from his outstretched hands and slipped it around my neck, not stopping to think about where it had just been until after the fact.

"You're the reason hurricanes are named after people, *Soldier.*" I left the insolent man with that little barb and walked toward the back door.

Where am I going? Chance's deep laugh pulled me back to reality. I turned and marched right up to the boulder of a man who may have once intimidated me, but now was just irritating me.

"Enjoy that, did you?" My eyebrows had long since disappeared into my hairline and I stood, one hip jutted out as I waited for his reply.

"Oh, honey. More than you know."

Another roll of the eyes and a hair flip for good measure reminded me *who* I was and *why* I was there. I was a Walker, of the Georgia Walkers. And I'd be damned if I was going to stand around being insulted by a man elbow deep in soap bubbles.

Bennett whisked past us, in search of a different, *unclaimed* apron, and I couldn't help but notice his piney, manly scent that lingered on the fabric of the apron. How, after only a few encounters, was I connecting that smell to the handsome, bearded derelict that just walked by? And why did it give my heart an unwelcome little jump? *Princess Jillian indeed.*

Chapter 9

Bennett

"SO, SOLDIER, I haven't seen you around lately." Her chipper tone was masking something else. Accusation, maybe? Chance assigned Jillian and me to the buffet line, so we stood side by side at the edge of a full to bursting dining room, serving food with the expertise of two old ladies working the lunch rush at Luby's. She was serving steaming green beans with bits of bacon in them and I was slicing brisket with an electric knife, but we were in close enough proximity for small talk.

"Wow, Princess. If that's the best pickup line you've got, you'll never find your prince." Teasing her was fun. Maybe a little too much fun. There were few things I liked more than watching Jillian's cheeks explode from a light, golden tan to pomegranate, and that seemed to happen fairly often. Was it me or did that happen all the time?

"Oh my God, stop it. You know what I mean… " She talked from the side of her mouth in between serving up artificially sweetened smiles as she scooped beans onto the sectioned plates.

"You know, the first time I saw you here, I thought you were like *them*." Her chin jutted in the direction of the full dining room. "You know, a customer?"

"I'm not sure 'customer' is an accurate term." Most of these people hadn't been actual *customers* in a place this nice in a long time, myself included.

"Okay, *guest* then?"

I nodded. That seemed appropriate.

"Well, what if I told you I *was* a guest?" I continued to cut the smoked brisket as the line of people ambled past us, but I watched her from the corner of my eye. No reaction. I'd been around girls like Jillian Walker. The ranch where I spent my high school years fed into an incredibly well-off district. It was the kind of place where, if you didn't drive a BMW, it was only because Daddy gave you a Mercedes instead. One thing about the rich and spoiled; they all seemed to buy their personalities from the same factory. But instinct told me this girl was different.

"I guess I'd lose respect for you, taking handouts like that. This organization was built for the *community*, not for students."

Chance relieved me of my meat cutting duties, so I grabbed a big metal spoon and took up residence at the potato salad—same distance from the princess, just on the opposite side. "I heard you, you know. A few weeks back, talking to Chance out in the parking lot? I heard when you said that drifters and bums were just taking advantage of him."

I continued serving, as if I'd just spoken of the weather. She continued too, mask firmly in place. But I could tell my overhearing their conversation made her uncomfortable, a fact I found encouraging. Maybe I was right and she wasn't a Stepford daughter.

"So, what's your point?" She played it cool.

"I just want you to know you're wrong. These people," with an open hand, I swept my hand across the room, encompassing everybody, "the ones in this room, each have a story. If point A is a safe, secure life and point B is having to rely on the generosity of strangers to survive, these people can tell you there are many paths from one to the other. They aren't here by choice, not really."

She tilted her head in my direction, a snarky snort escaping her smirking lips. If I had to guess, I'd say the noise was automatic, involuntary. She was too classy to lose control like that.

"You'll never convince me of that." Superiority and entitlement could be such ugly accessories. They could ruin even the most beautiful of creatures.

"You wanna make a bet?" That was the army talking. With very little by way of entertainment, we gambled. *On* anything and *with* anything. Lots of guys had women back home and they'd send cookies and candy. One guy even got tiny little bottles of Jack Daniel's since his lady worked for the airlines. Once a month, that guy was *everyone's* best friend.

"What are you mumbling about?" She grabbed her empty bean tray and headed for the kitchen. All the people had come through and were busy eating and chatting with each other, giving us the green light to start breaking things down and getting them clean. I grabbed my almost-empty tray and followed her.

"A bet. You know, a bet? I tell you I can do something and then we put stakes on it. If I succeed, I get this, and if I don't, I have to give you that." Only this time, we wouldn't be playing for MREs and mustard packets.

She rolled her eyes. "I know what a bet is, jackass. So what is it you want to bet on?" She grabbed the sprayer and started hosing out the stainless steel container with vigor. Her attempts to seem unaffected at my standing so close were unsuccessful. She licked her lips and avoided eye contact, but still stood with a confidence that couldn't be bought for any price.

"I bet that I can change your mind... about those people out there. Give me," grabbing a number off the top of my head, "four weeks and I bet I can change your opinion of the guests that come here."

She flipped the water off and returned the nozzle to its hook, then spun around, crossing her arms over her chest and cocking one eyebrow like she'd done so many times tonight. "And if you don't?"

"If I don't change your mind after four weeks, I'll never touch your apron again."

She laughed, big and strong, before sending a pointed look in my direction and waving a perfectly manicured finger inches from my face. "Oh, you'll *never* touch my apron again no matter how this plays out, but I'm intrigued. You forgot to mention one thing, though." If her laugh had been a song, I'd play it again and again until I couldn't get it out of my head.

"What's in this for you? What happens if you succeed?" She'd included air quotes around that last part and it should have pissed me off. But it didn't. It was almost cute.

"Well, if... no, *when* I succeed... you help serve Thanksgiving dinner here, at the cafe." I felt my heart beating in my throat and wondered if she could tell, and for a moment, I begged the words to jump back into my mouth. But it was out there, and couldn't be unsaid, so imagine my surprise when she offered up one little word.

"Deal."

Chapter 10

Jillian

THAT INSUFFERABLE MAN and his damn bet. I hadn't seen Gareth in months and had only spoken with him a handful of times since he started at Harvard Law. Thanksgiving was going to be our chance to be together again… to rekindle the romance of last year when he was a senior and we were together all the time. There was no way I was letting Thanksgiving slip through my fingers. But I wasn't worried. This was easy. I was in complete control.

"Now, remember. You're not here to grill them. You're just here to befriend them. When they trust you, they'll open up and share some of their stories." I slapped him on the arm.

"I'm not an idiot, Mr. Hanson. I've dined with presidents and foreign dignitaries. Vagabonds ought to be a piece of cake after that." Bennett slapped his forehead. *What did I say?*

We'd agreed to meet for dinner at the cafe on Wednesday nights. Never mind that Bennett had a late class on Mondays… there was *no way* I was going to miss my sorority's weekly chapter meeting to hang out with people who couldn't be bothered to help themselves. And Friday was my night to volunteer. And now his too, apparently. My mysterious Friday night absences from Greek social events had not gone unnoticed. Plenty of perfectly manicured eyebrows had been raised in my direction lately.

For the most part, I'd held it together, but I had a mild panic attack at the thought of actually dining with real street people. When I expressed my concern, Bennett assured me that he would keep me safe. He'd set this all up, but I still didn't trust him.

"Before we go in, tell me. How do you know these people?" He stopped on the front porch of the cafe and turned to look at me.

"I spend a lot of time here. It's kind of my hangout now." Okay, loser. Time to get new friends if you're hanging out at the local soup kitchen for companionship. Of course, I didn't say that, my bitch filter firmly in place. I nodded with my pleasant smile also firmly in place.

Entering through the front doors felt weird. Other than the absence of a cash register, there was nothing to indicate this wasn't just a typical Southern mom-and-pop joint you'd find in any little town. It was a sweet place, minus the clientele. The same clientele I would soon be dining with.

Grabbing a plate and helping myself to scrambled

eggs and bacon on a tortilla topped with salsa and cheese felt like the Twilight Zone. I was on the other side of the serving line. I was breaking bread with *them*. And there were no words to describe what was going through my mind as I sat down next to a woman who didn't look much older than me, with two small children flanking her, already digging in. I gasped when I glanced down and saw that she was incredibly pregnant.

"Rosalinda Macias, I'd like to introduce you to Jillian Walker. Jillian, meet Rosalinda and her daughters, Gabby and Ari." The two girls (one I'd place around eight years old and the other about two) both shared their mother's wide, black eyes and thick eyelashes. The girls' long, straight black hair was artfully braided and the older one, Gabby, had a wilted dandelion flower tucked behind one ear. They were beautiful, all three of them, and clean. I was surprised.

"Hello there." The look on my face must have been priceless. The young mother stared at me like I was wearing a turtle as a hat. "Howwww arrrrre youuuuuuu?" What *was* this slow, loud voice coming out of me? I felt possessed.

Bennett noticed it too. He poked me in the ribs and casually whispered, "Rosalinda is from the Panhandle, not Mexico. Talk to her like she's human, not something that just deboarded a flying saucer." He then turned to Rosalinda, whose soft smile indicated she'd heard every word. "Sorry about my friend here. She doesn't get out much."

My eyes rolled back in my head, which earned a giggle from the older girl. It took everything in me not to slap him for that, but I remained calm, for the sake of the children.

So, what now? The woman looked at me. I looked at the woman. Eating dinner with poor people was a lot easier in theory than it was in reality. When I had dinner with someone, it was because we were alike in some way. There was some common ground, a jumping-off point. Something. This woman was nothing like me at all, but what about her daughter?

"So, Gabby, what are you reading?" I pulled out an orange painted wooden chair and sat down beside her. The young girl didn't look old enough to read anything, much less the chapter book her nose was buried in. When she didn't respond, Rosalinda elbowed her, and her sheepish look told me becoming lost in the world within the pages was a common occurrence. She glanced at me, then looked to her mother for silent approval before speaking to me directly.

"It's called *Trumpet of the Swan*. In my class, we're reading *Charlotte's Web*, but since I've already read that one a few times, my teacher let me choose another book by the same author."

I scooted closer. I could talk about books all day. "You know, this was one of my favorite books when I was a child. My mom actually hid it from me because every time I read it, I begged her to get me a swan." She laughed out loud and I noticed most of her teeth were capped in silver.

"I would have asked for a trumpet." Her simple smile warmed my heart. In truth, I *had* asked for a trumpet and my parents had gotten me one. I think I used it for decor. I certainly never learned to play like Louis, the main character, from the book about a trumpeter swan with no voice.

"I read, I read." Ari reached into a bag sitting at her feet and pulled out some white paper stapled together to resemble a book. On the cover was a bright drawing made in crayon. It appeared the other pages were a combination of pictures and words.

"What is that?" I was curious.

"Gabby writes books for Ari. She illustrates them and staples them together at school so she can read like her sister."

Why didn't they just get Ari her own books? I knew they made books for babies her age. I watched as the tiny girl's finger slid across the page, mouthing words. At one point, she stopped and laughed out loud. I had no idea what story was playing in her head, but whatever it was, it must have been hilarious. Rosalinda looked at her girls with such pride.

"What sweet girls you have."

Rosalinda smiled.

"Thank you. Yes, they are sweet. And I pray every night that they can make something of themselves. My worst nightmare is that they make the same mistakes I did." Her words were scarcely more than a whisper, but the pain in her eyes screamed.

"Hey now, none of that." Bennett piped in. "Remember what we talked about last week?"

Gabby popped up from her book. "You said to always look forward, never look back."

"And why should you never look back?" I asked. This just got interesting.

"Mr. Ben says if you don't look forward, you'll never find your second chance."

I'm not sure what I was expecting to come out of the pretty little girl with the really big brain, but it certainly wasn't that.

"Very good Gabby! At least *someone* was listening." Bennett's words were meant for Gabby, but aimed at Rosa… but in a gentle, playful tone and I could easily picture him as a father, teasing his own daughter in that way. This was a very different side to the strong, unassuming man and not at all unwelcome. His softer side only added to his mystery. One that I had no business solving.

Rosalinda blushed and patted Bennett's shoulder, then turned toward her little girls. "Hey mija, I think Ms. Lillie might have something for you and your sister.

Why don't you two run over and see what she's got over there?" Her words were strained, and I have no doubt Gabby caught on, but she slid her bookmark into place and both girls jumped up and scurried off in search of whatever sweet treat Lillie Lowe had in her magical basket. When they were out of earshot, she leaned in closer to Bennett, who'd taken a seat next to her.

"He called again this weekend." Rosalinda's voice shook as she twisted a paper napkin to shreds. Bennett was leaning forward, elbows propped on his knees with his hands steepled in front of his mouth.

"What did he want?" Rosalinda snorted.

"To come home, of course. What does he always want?"

"And what did you say?" It was like they were the only two in the room. Did he even remember I was there, growing more and more uncomfortable by the second? I should have excused myself, but it was like an accident on the side of the road: too intriguing to look away, or in my case, *walk* away.

"I did exactly what you said. I told him to go to hell. Then, I called the police, locked my doors, and prayed to St. Michael to keep us safe from harm. Turns out, he was calling from jail. He's suspected of armed robbery." She sat up, pressing her back against her chair as a slow smile crept across their faces. Then, they high fived.

I waved as a reminder of my presence. "Clearly, I'm missing something here." Ben raised his eyebrows toward the woman who was wiping tears from her eyes. Signaled by a slight nod of her head, he turned my way.

"Rosa's ex, Armando, is the scum of the earth. While Rosa worked two jobs to afford their small apartment, Mando took what little was left and gambled it away. When Rosa wasn't able to pay all the bills, he took his angry displeasure of the situation out on her face."

I was appalled, and wondered if it showed on my face. I quickly schooled my features, just like I'd been taught. "So, why the celebration?"

"Oh. This weekend, the dirt bag was picked up for armed robbery. If convicted, which he will be, right Rosa?" She nodded emphatically. "That will make his third felony and in Texas, there's a 'Three Strikes' law. No bail, no probation, no leniency. Just prison. Exactly where the bastard should be."

Rosalinda's face lit up like a Christmas tree at Bennett's words, and while new tears started to slide down her face, these were tears of pure joy. How long had Bennett known this woman? And what was his role in her life? I didn't get the vibe they were involved romantically, but they were definitely closer than two people who just met at a soup kitchen. Then it dawned on me. I really didn't know much about Bennett Hanson at all.

The rest of the meal was spent discussing Gabby's excellent grades and the books she'd read. We also spoke of Rosa's pregnancy and how it would affect her income. She didn't seem too worried. She had a plan that included a strong support system, but of course Bennett offered to help in any way he could. It was a lovely evening and the little family of three, soon four, was full of life.

"So, are they homeless?" I asked, needing to know more. We were walking back to campus, where I'd left my car. My Wednesday afternoon class was just a few blocks away from the cafe, so it made the most sense to walk.

"No, they aren't homeless. They rent a room from her aunt. Or maybe great-aunt? Cousin? I can't really remember, but they only have kitchen privileges a few nights a week. So, on the nights she can't cook for her family, they come here."

"But, doesn't she work? Couldn't they just eat out or get an apartment with a kitchen they didn't have to share?" The idea of that woman having to share one room with those two little girls was unsettling. And with a baby on the way? It was unfathomable. She had to know this wasn't an ideal situation and at least try to make it better.

Bennett stopped mid-stride. "Do you have any idea what the average rent is in this city? I know it's not a booming metropolis like Houston or Dallas, but it's a college town. The apartment complexes and condos cater to the average college student, driving to school in their brand-new Firebird or Jetta, armed with their daddy's checkbook and just enough sense to get up in the morning." He rolled his eyes and my mind went directly to my top desk drawer, where I kept *my* daddy's checkbook. He was absolutely right and I should have viewed his comments as a personal affront. But how could I?

"You know, the real world is hard enough, but pile a couple of kids on top and it's that much harder. When they lost the apartment because she wasn't 'working hard enough,' they came home to changed locks. They had nothing but the clothes on their backs. But Rosalinda never gave up, never stopped looking for a better life for her girls. Right now, that room in her aunt's house is paradise. It's in a decent neighborhood, with decent schools, and she doesn't have to fear for their safety."

We walked in comfortable silence, as dusk settled into night and the air grew cooler. How did one rebuild from nothing, especially with two kids and one on the way? What would become of them?

"How do they get to the cafe?" The question was out before I could stop it, but I was particularly curious. It always amazed me how full the cafe could be with only a half-empty parking lot. Where did they come from?

"I had that same question. When they opened the place, Chance had it put on the city bus schedule. Look out the side window about twenty minutes before the doors open. It's almost the entire bus that gets off on that corner. Rosa and her kids use it."

"No car then?" Bennett shook his head. My mind was reeling after everything I'd seen and heard. How did I not know these people existed? And how many were there?

"You met her at the cafe, right?" Bennett nodded. "When?"

"Let's see." His gaze drifted up as if he were viewing a calendar in his brain. "I guess about three weeks ago?" I stopped.

"So, in three weeks, you got her whole life story?" He nodded again. My head was cocked to the side as I viewed him with scrunched up eyes. When I realized what I was doing, I steadied my face. "But why? Why would someone with, I assume major trust issues, let you in on the intricacies of their life?" I just couldn't understand.

He shrugged his shoulders. "I don't know. It's just what people do."

Huh. It's just what people do? I pondered his words as we walked across some green space between buildings. *It's just what people do.* He was right. So many times, I'd caught myself with my defenses down. There was something about his wide eyes, relaxed smile, and smooth baritone voice that lured me in. And it was also something that could get me in a lot of trouble if I wasn't careful.

"Hey, you okay?" The words pulled me from my trance and I noticed I was stopped at a crosswalk that was blinking at me to cross within the next seventeen seconds.

"Oh, yeah. Sorry. I just have a test tomorrow and I was thinking about everything I need to study." That was a lie in its purest form, but there was no way I'd admit that he had my full attention. There was no way I was opening up to this smooth operator. And forget giving in and spending Thanksgiving here. "This is my parking garage." I veered right and he stopped.

"So, I'll see you Friday?" I nodded, he tipped his chin up in response, and we parted ways.

The entire drive home, which included stopping for the world's longest and loudest train, my mind was fixated on Rosalinda. She was probably the strongest woman I'd ever known. But upon meeting her, no one would ever guess she'd been a victim of domestic abuse, homeless, and destitute all within the last twelve months, because her smile told a different story; one of happiness, love, and hope.

Chapter 11

Bennett

THE NEXT 48 hours were spent alternating between studying what I needed to pass my classes, and reading anything I could get my hands on about Combat Stress Reaction, or what the shrinks were now calling Post-Traumatic Stress Disorder.

In combat, soldiers learn real quick how to suppress emotions. There's just too much other baggage to handle without putting feelings into the mix. And, I think it's a way to help soldiers come to terms with the idea that death could be just around the corner. Any normal guy off the street would run away screaming if shots were being fired at him, but for us, it was just another day at the office.

But burying all that fear and guilt came with a consequence and I was living it. The molten lava of all that suppressed emotion was bubbling to the surface, ready to erupt, and I was powerless to stop it.

Truth is, I felt safer, more like myself, in combat. There, I could hide behind weapons and ammunition. Had it not been for that day in the desert a little more than eighteen months earlier, I'd probably still be there. Fighting the war out there was much easier than fighting the one inside my soul. There, the bad guy was tangible, real. Right now, I was my own worst enemy. I was living in past tense and it was time for me to come to the present.

Caught up with the latest research done by a psychiatrist in England, I glanced at my watch and popped up, dropping the journal on the floor with a thud.

"Damn it!"

It was Friday, and I was late, so I ran the half mile from the library to the cafe and got there just as the doors were opening.

"You're late." Mrs. Lowe smiled, taking in my disheveled state.

"Very observant. Be right back." I left her serving what looked to be chicken spaghetti in the dining room to wash my hands and prepare to get my volunteer on. Nodding to a few others I recognized as I walked through the kitchen, I found my apron and headed back out.

Where is she? Automatically, my eyes scanned the growing crowd for Jillian. Why? I wasn't too sure I was ready to deep dive into that question, but here I was, looking high and low, and not finding her anywhere.

"She's over there." I glanced up at Chance, his

Cheshire grin larger than life.

"*She* who? I'm not looking for a *she*." *Liar, liar, pants on fire.*

Thunderous laughter rumbled out of the older man's mouth and I rolled my eyes. "Okay, man." He clapped me on the shoulder, shaking his head. "And I bet if you tell yourself that long enough, you might actually start to believe it." More laughter followed as he walked away.

I turned the direction she was and saw her sitting on the floor, holding Ari Macias in her lap, while engaged in an animated conversation with Gabby. Ari's head was resting on her shoulder as the little girl played with the string of silver beads around Jillian's neck. If I had to guess, she and Gabby were discussing books, which she did successfully all while playing with the baby's hair. Her face was so relaxed when she thought no one was watching. I always felt as if she were putting on a show with me. Now, watching the real Jillian, she was breathtaking.

As she talked, she scanned the room a few times before she finally found me. Our eyes locked for the briefest of seconds and the corners of her mouth turned up for a quick moment, but it was fleeting. She had obviously been well-schooled in getting her emotions under control. Back to her conversation as if that little smile hadn't been just for me, I saw the apples of her cheeks redden and for some odd reason, I took great pride in that.

"Can I walk you to your car?" She nodded.

"Sure, just let me put my apron up and grab my purse. Be right back." After a calm night and a quick cleanup, we were getting out a little earlier than expected. While I waited, the Lowes came out of the kitchen, Mrs. Lowe laughing at something her husband was saying.

"Bennett, why are you still here, boy? It's Friday night! Shouldn't you be out with some pretty thing on your arm?" Mrs. Lowe grabbed my arm, pulling me out the front door.

"Lillie, you need to let that boy be. Besides, if I'm not mistaken, in about thirty seconds I'm guessing your wish will come true." And as if timed by Hollywood, Jillian came barreling out from the back.

"Sorry, Bennett. I'm ready to go now." She hadn't realized I wasn't alone. She stopped short and her blush returned, seeing the knowing smiles of the older couple. "No, this is not what it looks—"

"It's okay, Jillian." I jumped in, grabbing her arm and guiding her out the door. "The Lowes aren't interested in the romantic side of our relationship." Unable to contain my grin, I watched Jillian's gaze volley between their eyes and mine, her silent mouth opening and closing like a goldfish as I dragged her down the sidewalk. We walked about a hundred yards before she said anything.

"Why did you do that?" She definitely wasn't happy, but mad was the wrong word. Maybe, annoyingly curious?

"Do what, Princess?" I answered, feigning innocence. She made it too easy.

"Why did you make them think we were dating? And don't call me that. It's patronizing." A cold front had blown in and the cold October wind bit through the thin shirt I'd put on this morning when it was seventy-five degrees. Jillian felt it too, but tried to mask her discomfort. Why did she always try to appear so perfect and in control? It's like she viewed vulnerability as a poison. But, I thought, didn't we all?

"Bennett? Hey, Ben! Over here." We both turned our attention to the frantically waving brunette huddled with other versions of herself at the bus stop across the street. The girl waved her friends on and ran toward us.

"Hey, Ben." Her voice purred as she slinked toward us like a cat. Jillian and I had stopped in the middle of the sidewalk, our conversation halted for the moment.

"Darcy, right?" *Darcy? Marcy? Macy? Kasey? What was it?*

"Oh, you remembered. Good boy." *What was I, a dog?*

She sidled up beside me and grabbed my bicep, both of her tiny manicured hands barely able to wrap around it. "It's so cold out here."

I nodded. She was right, it was cold. And as if my nod was an invitation, the girl eased in a little closer. Maybe *she* was the dog. She reminded me of the blue heelers Doc kept on the ranch. Sometimes, he'd throw them a bone and they'd slobber all over themselves to get to it.

"Hey, it's not too late and you don't look busy. Do you wanna come to my place and study for the psych test next week? I have a fireplace. We could… *warm up*." She flashed a million-dollar smile as she waited expectantly for my answer. Beside me, Jillian guffawed, probably at her 'you don't look busy' comment.

"Oh, um… " It was Friday night. I was walking Jillian to her car. Then I was going home. I had to admit, it took balls to come on to someone with such fervor while a much more attractive girl stood not a foot away. Sure, she was just a friend, if I could even call her that. But Miss Priss didn't know that, which made me like her even less. Still, this was not something I'd expected and a blind man could read between the lines and know that studying was the *last* thing on her mind. I startled when my other bicep was seized and a hand shot out from beside me.

"Oh, hi." The inflection in her voice made me cringe. It screamed, *back off, bitch*, and it seemed to come naturally to Jill. "It's nice to meet one of Ben's school friends. Darcy, was it? Hmmm, he's never mentioned you. Ever. Anyway, I'm Jillian Walker."

If Darcy was a dog drooling over a bone, Jillian was the alpha, baring gums and teeth, along with a low growl. She was prepared to protect her territory. I shivered. Darcy must have felt it too. She took Princess's hand and the lust-filled smile melted off her pale, over made face as she sized Jillian up. No comparison. None. Checkmate. Matchpoint. Pack it up and go back to your friends, chick.

"Oh, well." She squirmed in place and looked at me, then to Jillian again, who was holding her hand much longer than was comfortable. And if I were to guess, her grip was probably much tighter than necessary, too. "It's nice to meet you. I guess I should go, I think I hear the bus." She wrenched her hand from Jillian's and scuttled back to her hive of overdressed, overly hairsprayed friends without a backward glance.

Jillian started walking again while I just stared. Actually, 'walking' may be too weak a term. Her pace made what we'd been doing just moments before seem like a casual stroll compared to the speed walking she was now doing.

"What the hell was that?" I asked as I caught up with her after a few beats. I had to admit, the events of the last few minutes had been funny as hell, and I very much appreciated her coming to my aid while I floundered like a fish out of water, but it was only natural to question her motivation.

"What? Certainly, you didn't want to go with that bimbo, to her house of sin and debauchery under the guise of studying, while she, and possibly her crew of Barbie girl, airheaded friends pawed all over you. Or did you?" I laughed.

"Not particularly, but I could have handled it. It's not like that's the first time I've been hit on." She stopped again and turned back toward me.

"What do you mean?" Her cute little head was cocked to one side and a deep wrinkle appeared between her eyebrows. Was it really that unbelievable that I would occasionally gain the attention of the fairer sex? I should have been offended, but I wasn't.

"Hey, what can I say? This is a military school… chicks dig soldiers." I shrugged. "It happens occasionally."

"*How* occasionally?" Her arms were crossed tight over her chest. She wasn't moving until she got her answer.

"A few times a week?"

"Define *a few*." Now her hands were on her hips. *Adorable*.

"Six or seven?" Her mouth gaped open.

"You get hit on that aggressively six or seven times a

week?" I chuckled.

"You think that was aggressive? That's nothing. I found a pair of silk undies in my backpack the other day with a phone number written on them and a few have gotten a little handsy with the goods, if you know what I mean. Now *that* qualifies as aggressive." Closing her eyes, she shook her head and with a huff, started walking again. When we arrived outside the garage where her car was parked, she stopped, but hesitated.

"What?" I wanted to know what was going on in that privileged little brain of hers.

"I'm just wondering, have you ever taken any of them up on their offers?"

I took a deep breath, burying my hands in my pockets, where I found the photo scrap tucked away. I flipped the corner of it with my fingers and, refusing to meet her eyes, I shook my head, hoping to avoid where this conversation was headed.

"Why not?" Looking up, her eyes bore holes into mine, like she was searching for the answer deep inside my soul. What should I tell her? That I wasn't interested in girls? No, that would be a lie. That I wasn't interested in a relationship? Well, that was true, to an extent, but I had no desire to tell her the real reason I didn't date—the same reason I would never enter into a serious relationship or get married. That was my burden, my weight to carry, my souvenir from that ill-fated day in the desert.

"Look, I'm here to study and get a degree. I won't let anything or anyone get in the way of that." The corners of her mouth turned down just a little and I felt it in my chest. She wasn't satisfied with my answer, almost as if she knew there was a truckload of baggage behind my words. But with a quick nod of her head, telling me she'd accepted my answer, for now, she turned and headed into the garage.

Chapter 12

Jillian

"AWW, LOOK AT THEM." I pointed at the two older people, all bundled up against the crisp afternoon air, as they wandered up the sidewalk. They held hands like it was their first date and the man's gentle laughter at something his wife said melted my heart a little more.

"Yeah. Adorable." Bennett deadpanned. "They're actually our dinner companions this evening." At the rate they were walking, we wouldn't get to dinner until midnight.

We'd made it to Wednesday and round two of the bet. And already, my dream Thanksgiving with my dreamy boyfriend was feeling a bit threatened. Because, I planned to stick to my word. Waiting in front of the cafe, I took advantage of Ben's distraction and checked him out. He wore that same grey T-shirt and at first glance, his jeans were nothing special. But from behind, he wore those Wranglers like he was doing them a favor and I suddenly became aware that I was practically panting.

Bennett, ever the gentleman, held the door as the

couple strolled in and took a seat. We followed, but almost immediately, Mrs. Lowe placed small plates of pasta with steaming meat sauce in front of the couple. She shook the old man's gnarled hand and gently hugged the woman, taking her coat to hang on one of the hooks by the door.

"Bernadette, Willie, this is Jillian, my, um, friend." He presented me like I was a new car being offered on *The Price is Right*. "Jillian, it's my pleasure to introduce you to Bernadette and Willie Coleson."

I offered my hand and both of them shook it gently, the gentleman offering me a seat. "Here, you sit young lady, and let Bennett go rustle you up some spaghetti." Bennett nodded, taking his cue to leave, and whisked off, leaving me alone with members of the Golden Girls cast.

"It's so nice of you to join us for dinner this evening." Mrs. Coleson's smile was bright and her voice was so soothing. It made me want to crawl into her lap and ask her to read me stories. "So, dear, tell us about yourself." Me? We weren't here to talk about me!

"Yes, ma'am. Well, I'm originally from Georgia."

"I can tell by the accent. What brought you west?" While Mrs. Coleson asked all the questions, Mr. Coleson tasked himself with cutting up her pasta. When he finished, he sprinkled a bit of parmesan cheese over the top and buttered her garlic toast.

"Oh, I decided to come to Texas A&M because—," I stopped. Why *had* I come to A&M? It was simple. Because of a boy. I came to Texas A&M because, since before I could talk, I'd been told that I would marry Gareth Johnson and I came to Texas A&M to solidify that arrangement. Why was I just now realizing that? And why were my eyes locked on Bennett, walking toward our table with two plates of pasta and two salads balanced precariously in his arms? I shook my head. "I'm sorry, I came to Texas A&M to spread my wings." Bennett presented my food with a flourish, as a waiter would at a high-end restaurant, before taking his seat next to me. He neatly placed his napkin in his lap and waited for me to pick up my fork before picking his up.

"That's so nice. This is a wonderful place to live and raise a family. Do you think you'll stay here, once you marry?" How could I tell them that, most likely, I'd be receiving mail at 1600 Pennsylvania Avenue before it was all said and done? I couldn't, not when I didn't fully believe it myself.

"Oh, I haven't really thought about the long term. There'll be plenty of time to think about that later. I'm only twenty." Heat creped up my cheeks and I concentrated on my food.

"Well, by the time I was twenty, I'd already buried one husband and was being courted by husband number two." She elbowed a silent Willie in the ribs as Bennett passed me the parmesan cheese.

"I'd've been husband number one if you'd said yes the first time I asked you." He harrumphed, digging into his spaghetti. She just batted his words away with a roll of her eyes and a grin on her lips.

"Oh, don't listen to him. The first time he asked me was on the playground at Bowie Elementary School. The boy had no shoes on and not a moment before, he'd been making bets with the other boys to see how many rocks they could sneak into the building between their   toes."

"I was the champion. No one could beat me." He continued eating, like he'd never said a word. I cast a quick glance at Bennett and caught him looking at me, amusement painted across his face.

"When I came of age, Willie was off fighting a war in France. He'd followed his older brother over there and I figured he'd never come back." She sighed, wistfully lost in her memories.

"Yeah, so she married my *younger* brother."

Wait, what? I swung my head around in question, but Bennett's quick wink said he'd heard it all before.

"Okay, so fine. I married his brother. The boy had flat feet and the army had no use for him."

Her husband huffed again, never looking up, but nothing about his demeanor spoke of anger. "Willie was the one I wanted, but I just figured he wasn't coming back, so I married Ronald." She shivered at the thought. Ronald must have been a real sour lemon judging by the looks on both Bernadette's and Willie's faces.

"But tell them what happened to Ronald, Bernie."

She rolled her eyes and sucked her teeth, giving me a little glimpse of myself a hundred years from now. "Ronald, unbeknownst to me, had a faulty moral compass and a peculiar take on marriage and monogamy. He also had an interesting relationship with the truth. Just a few hours after the ceremony, the imbecile fell ill and never recovered. He'd contracted syphilis from God knows where and let me tell you, it was a blessing. I don't think his own mother even cried."

"But, why?" Who was this Ronald character? Willie was all too happy to chime in.

"He was a monster from the day he was born. He came out causing trouble and never stopped. Oh, sure. He was a charmer in the light of day, but integrity is what you do when no one else is watching, and that boy didn't have an ounce."

"Oh, my." I hadn't expected such a tragic, yet satisfying ending. Because, of course, Bernadette and Willie deserved their happily ever after that had started with dirty feet on the school playground.

"And then, before the body was even cold, my

soldier boy came home to me. So you see, if I hadn't married Ronald, I may have married someone even more scrupulous and then where would we be?" Willie continued eating, but he sat a little taller when Bernadette placed her hand on his.

"So, if you don't mind me asking," I shot a look at Bennett, but he nodded for me to continue, "what brings you two here, to The Community Cafe?"

"Well, the Good Lord never blessed us with children, though I stayed home day in and day out praying for a miracle. That's what women did back then. So, I kept the home fires burning while Willie here taught history at the high school. But after two hip replacements, he had to hang up his hat. And I'll tell you what, it's a might tight, two people living on one teacher's retirement. The cafe is only three blocks away from our house, and walking down here three days a week is not only good exercise, but smart business. It cuts our grocery bill nearly in half." The couple smiled, as if they'd just let me in on the secret to life. And maybe they had.

Because there I sat, astonished. These two people had nothing but each other in this world. And while my heart ached for their circumstance, they didn't seem bothered in the least. This was their normal, same with Rosalinda. They weren't constantly trying to climb their way to something better, rather they appreciated what they had. What a change from what I'd grown up with.

"And what about family? Do you have anyone to go visit, or someone who visits you?" These two were peas and carrots and my greatest fear now was… what happens when one of them dies?

"All of my people are long gone, but Willie's older brother Anthony has kids, grandkids, and great-grandkids. We aren't close, but one of his great-granddaughters is in school here and she visits from time to time, though come to think of it, we haven't seen much of her this fall."

Bernadette turned to Willie and asked, "When was the last time Lori stopped by, do you remember?"

Lori?

"Oh, well." He paused in the way old men do when they're thinking extra hard. "I suppose it was when she brought that boy around." Willie turned and addressed me directly. "It's the darndest thing. She comes 'round to introduce us to her new beau, and I think he said he was somehow related to the governor." His wide grin revealed a few missing teeth. "Isn't that something?"

My heart dropped into my stomach. Yeah. That was something, all right.

I was quiet for the rest of the meal, trying to piece together why Lori and Gareth would have been together and why they would give the Colesons reason to suspect they were anything other than childhood

115

friends. None of it made sense.

"They were sweet." I bundled up, combatting the frigid wind that came with early November. And though I wasn't quite ready to admit defeat, I had to admit that things were changing inside of me.

"Aren't they? And just as pure as the day is long." We walked out to my car and for the first time, Bennett had agreed to let me drive him to the library. He said he had some things to do before going home.

"It's sad that they never had children, but, kids or no kids, I hope to find a love like that one day."

Bennett sighed and buckled his seatbelt. "Don't we all."

Still no message on the answering machine from Gareth. I tried his apartment again and left the same message I'd been leaving for weeks. "Hey, it's Jillian. Call me back." It was only upon hanging up that I realized I'd left out the part where I usually said I loved and missed him.

Chapter 13

Bennett

I HADN'T PLANNED to take a road trip until after finals, but in our weekly calls—what I refer to as the 'State of the Ranch' calls—Doc mentioned they had a good chance of ice the following week. I remembered preparing for a hard freeze on the ranch since I'd done it many times. At the moment, they'd taken a break from fostering and the absence of extra hands made the burden close to impossible for one person to shoulder. So Friday morning, I hopped on a Greyhound bus and headed north.

"Boy, are you a sight for sore eyes." Doc clapped me on the back before pulling me in for a hug. Displays of emotion were few and far between, but I know how worried they were after the attack. They've both been a lot more affectionate since I showed up on their doorstep six months ago.

"Good to see you too, old man." And it was. It was so good to see a familiar face and a familiar place. What had been lush, green grass was now turning brown, as were the leaves on the oaks, while the setting sun created a patchwork of golden light for miles. Fall at the ranch was something out of a dream. Maybe because when I first arrived, it had been fall and even my angsty teen self could appreciate beauty in the wide-open space, along with the freedom that it symbolized.

My caseworker called the ranch my *second chance*. But when had I been given a first chance? My parents were still children themselves when I was born. I hadn't been planned and they certainly didn't let parenthood get in the way of their sex, drugs, and rock 'n roll lifestyle. I spent many a night listening to my coked-up dad beat on my mom mercilessly, only to hear them making up ten minutes later.

Being placed with Doc and Rosie meant I had been given a new normal. I finally had an opportunity to be a kid for the first time in my life, and once I exorcised my demons through blood, sweat, and tears on the ranch, I did just that.

We rode along in amiable silence, as we'd done for close to ten years. If I was a man of few words, Doc was a man of even fewer, but it had been exactly what I needed back then. And maybe now, too.

In the beginning, when I'd come to the ranch with a chip on my shoulder the size of the Titanic, Doc took one look at me and put me to work. We labored, side by side for hours, then days, not exchanging more than a handful of words. Then, one day the silence got to me and I started talking. I talked and I talked, and I talked some more. I ranted and raved. I screamed and I shouted. I swore, and I cried and soon enough, I'd gotten it all out, all while Doc just kept working, and gifting me the occasional nod to let me know he was, in fact, listening.

I asked him about it years later. I asked him why he stayed silent, while I blamed the universe, the world, my parents, and even him for all the problems in my life and I'll never forget what he said.

"Silence was my gift to you. What you'd been through broke my heart and so did knowing I couldn't change it. But I could listen. As a foster parent, there was very little I could do to fix the broken boy in front of me, but that boy didn't need fixing. He needed healing. And he had the strength to heal deep inside of him the whole time. All he had to do was let the bad stuff out so good stuff could replace it."

Of course, he was right. He always was. And

from then on, when I needed to 'let the bad stuff out,' I asked Doc if we needed to ride the fence line. Sometimes he'd extend an invite if he thought something was troubling me. That was our code and I had a feeling we'd be checking a lot of fences the next few days.

"Bravo!" Rosie squealed as I snuck up behind her and swung her around the kitchen. She was losing weight. That worried me.

"Surprise." Up on her bare toes, she threw her arms around my neck for a tight squeeze, then held me by the shoulders at arm's length for inspection.

"You're too skinny," she chided, clicking her tongue. "You aren't eating." I started to shake my head, but thought better of it. She wanted the truth, but there was no way I'd tell her most of my money was here, invested in this house, this ranch. She'd murder me if she knew how little I kept to live on.

"Well, that's why I'm here! Nothing compares to your cooking. Feed me woman, feed me!" Her stare held me in place, her face stone-cold sober. She didn't buy it. But that was too bad. It was all she was getting.

"Why are you here, mijo?"

"Doc mentioned a hard freeze. Thought I'd help him get things ready."

"Why are you *really* here?" She dropped her arms and I backed up until I was leaning against the butcher block island where I'd spent countless hours doing homework while Rosie fussed around the kitchen. "It's that girl."

Damn that woman and her Mexican voodoo.

"Mama, this again?" I turned to the sink and washed the travel nastiness off my hands. It also justified turning my back on Rosie. Her eyes had fangs that could sink right into my soul and suck out the truth without me even realizing it.

"You love her… "

I closed my eyes and took a few deep breaths while I rinsed off the soap suds and dried my hands with a paper towel. Turning back around, I met those big, brown soul-searching eyes again. "Are you asking or telling?"

"Hmmm" is all she said. That usually translated into '*I'm going to let you figure this one out, then you tell me.*'

"Jesus, Mary, and Joseph, woman. What do you want from me?"

She'd been vigorously scrubbing an already immaculate countertop, but stopped at my words.

"La verdad."

I ran my hands through my too long hair, applying pressure to my skull as I did. But my headache wasn't in there, it was standing right in front of me, demanding I speak of things I had yet to even let myself think about.

"The truth? Okay, here's the truth. I met a girl. She's spoiled and narrow-minded, entitled and completely out of touch with reality. She's a princess."

"And?" *Dammit.*

"And she reminds me what it feels like to have a heartbeat."

It took half a day to check the electric waterers and move the hay closer to the feeding area. After a quick lunch of vegetable beef stew, I insulated the pipes on the house and the barn and tested the generator, while Doc checked the fence line in the grazing pasture. By three o'clock, not only was everything almost ready, but the cold front began shifting and it appeared it was all for naught. Still, the time spent working in the wide-open space, breathing in the crisp country air was better than any prescription for beating the blues.

"You know, she's not asking you to wife up. She just doesn't want you to be alone forever." I'd been poking around the barn, looking for an excuse to stay out a little longer and ended up rearranging tack that was perfectly organized to begin with.

"She meddles," was all I had to say about the matter. I was using the push broom to sweep up what looked to be a decade worth of dust from the tack room floor, dreading another round of The Third Degree with Rosie the Roper.

"She's sick, Ben."

The broomstick fell from my hands, but I never heard it hit the floor.

"It was a small lump, I had it removed. No big deal," she said, as if she was telling us she had to stop at the post office on the way home.

"No, not a big deal." My eyes rolled back into my head. I wasn't a moron. "Is that why you have no kids right now?" I looked from Rosie to Doc, but his eyes deferred back to his wife. "Is it? Because you have cancer?"

"Had cancer, Bennett. *Had*. Past tense." She stood and walked up the stairs, taking care that we heard every step she took until her bedroom door slammed. She seemed adamant, but I had my doubts.

"I've never seen her pissed off." I said to no one in

particular, looking in the direction she'd gone.

"She's not pissed, Ben. She's scared. The lump was removed right before you got home. She was treated with a chemotherapy that beat up on her white blood cell counts. She had to have blood booster shots after each treatment. Now, she's on tamoxifen and her prognosis is good."

"Wait. Before I got home? So, this summer, while I was home, Rosie was going through chemo?" He nodded.

"She didn't want you to know. She didn't want you to stay because of her. She wanted you to go to school and make a life for yourself."

The silence cast a shadow of shame upon my heart.

"Well, I better go check on her. She goes to bed pretty early these days, so once I get her settled, I'll come find you." I nodded, only half hearing him.

I'd been home all summer. I'd been working the land, riding the fence lines. I'd been drinking and I'd been running.

The saying, 'War changes people,' is often misunderstood. Its literal value isn't taken into account. War truly changes a person. It injects a blackness into their soul that changes who they are and what they will be forever. But that fall wasn't too far for me.

We are the sum of our experiences. And my formative years were spent in a home with a sociopathic monster. One who used his discontent to rationalize a level of brutality and violence most grown men couldn't stomach. His victim being a woman whose need to escape into her next fix burned like a fire in her soul.

During my time in the Middle East, my lack of empathy made me a brilliant soldier. I viewed the enemy as an infection threatening to spread if I didn't step up and defend my country. The day Chance took his first life, he spent the night puking into a latrine. My first kill was that same night and I slept like a baby.

That alone sealed my fate. I would be career military, like my mentor, Commander Daniel Daniels. Some kids enlisted, did their time, went home, and had a wife and a child within a year. That wasn't the life I was bred for. That desire for home and hearth was nonexistent for me. I was happiest on the battlefield. I belonged in the thick of it all. But that plan blew up in my face.

The plane ride home from Germany was my walk of shame. The US Army terminated our relationship with an, *It's not us, it's you*, and as a parting gift, offered a pity ride to Texas. So I arrived at the ranch to lick my wounds, and let alcohol replace food. When I no longer got drunk, I stopped drinking and I started trying to outrun invisible monsters, getting nowhere fast.

I unintentionally slept in Sunday morning. I had a bus to catch later that afternoon, but I had some things to say to Rosie and I was sure she had a few words for me as well.

"Ahh, he lives," she chided, flipping bacon and whipping eggs at the same time, like she had four arms. Mussed and unshaven, in only some green plaid pajama pants from Gap, I lumbered down the stairs and plopped onto the barstool I had always considered my own.

"Coffee." I dropped my head to the cool granite counter. I slept a good twelve hours and felt like I'd just competed in a triathlon. With the efficiency of a seasoned greasy spoon waitress, she whipped up a steaming mug of coffee within reach before I could doze back off. "Thanks," I grumbled.

"You're worried." It was a statement, not a question. I sat up and took a sip, burning my tongue.

"Well, yeah, I'm worried." *I'm not a robot.*

"Not about me though. Don't worry about me. I'll be fine." She believed it and I sort of did too. She was a tough old broad. I stood and hugged her from behind as she continued cooking.

"You're all I have," I whispered, choking up as the reality of losing her crashed into me like an asteroid to the chest.

"Bravo. Why?" She turned the burner off and the blue light under the skillet went dark. Then she turned to face me. "Why are you so against falling in love? Who is this girl, this *princess?*"

"She's… she's everything."

"And?" The honest truth? Did she really want to hear that? Did I?

"And I am nothing."

I'd gone and done the one thing I swore I'd never do.

I'd fallen for someone.

Chapter 14

Jillian

I'D BEEN IN A FUNK for days, and the root of it all was showing up for 'work' on Friday night to find that Bennett was out of town. His friendship, if one could call it that, was something I cherished and I physically felt his absence. So when Wednesday rolled around, I may have shown up for our dinner a few, or thirty, minutes early to find Bennett already there, waiting for me.

"Hi, stranger." I nodded, walking to where he sat on the concrete step behind the cafe.

"Princess." He tipped his head in acknowledgement as he stood, dusting himself off. Tonight he wore a faded pair of Levi's and a plaid shirt woven with greens and blues. It was a far cry from his usual cargo-style pants and black or grey T-shirts. And while the shirt was thicker to provide warmth, the jeans stuck to him like Saran Wrap in all the right places.

"Well, don't you look spiffy." I wiggled my eyebrows and saw color creep onto his cheeks. My heart was beating in my throat.

"Yeah, well. I grabbed some clothes from home over the weekend."

This was the first time I'd ever heard him talk about a 'home' and I wanted to know more, but later. We had a bet to tend to first.

"Tonight, you're going to meet Rafael and he's a little different than the others you've met so far. Raf had to leave a newborn son when he was drafted to fight in Vietnam. He was never quite the same after he returned, but he held it together for his son, Rafael Jr., or RJ. Last year, RJ took shrapnel to the chest and died before he could be lifted out. That's when things spun out of control for Raf."

We'd walked around to the front of the cafe, but stopped before entering the building, so Bennett could finish giving me his instructions. "He won't talk, and probably won't even look at you, but he's listening. And if he's got something to add, he will. Just be patient. This is a man who's had his heart broken again and again by fate. There's a lot to gain from someone who's lost so much."

The mood in the cafe was somber, or maybe it was just me. I'd been fed a lot of information on this particular case and I hadn't fully wrapped my head around it. Raf was easy to spot, huddled over a plate of enchiladas, beans, and rice like someone was going to take it from him. He was protecting his plate with his life.

I'd seen him once or twice before, and a month ago, the thought of eating with someone like Rafael would have sent me running for the hills, but now I was almost drawn to him.

"I'm going to go sit down, can you get my plate?" Bennett nodded, but the whole way over to Raf's table, he never took his eyes off me. Was he concerned for my safety? If I wasn't, he sure shouldn't be.

"I see you have an extra spot here. Do you mind if I sit down?" The man remained oblivious, hunkered down over his food, awkwardly gripping a fork in his left hand while occasionally shoveling some rice into his mouth like a feral child.

"Raf, my name is Jillian. I'm a friend of Bennett's. It sure is nice to meet you." He stiffened at the mention of his own name, but other than that one tiny flinch, he continued eating, so I decided to carry on a conversation with myself. We hadn't beaten the rush this time and the food line was long, so Bennett would be a while.

"I'm from Georgia, just outside of Atlanta, but you probably figured that out by my accent. Most people do. Have you ever been to Georgia? It's real nice, a lot like Texas with the heat and humidity. When I was a kid, I had two best friends, CJ and Jerome. I lived on a big plot of land and way toward the back, there was this creek that separated my lot from CJ's family estate. Luckily, someone had built a bridge between our two pieces of land. During the summers, we traveled that bridge so many times I knew every swollen, splintered board like an old friend. But sometimes, when it was just so hot you almost wanted to peel your skin right off, we'd skip the bridge altogether and go jump in that creek, clothes and all. I mean, of course I kept my clothes on, all my runnin' buddies were boys."

Raf had put his fork down and instead of staring straight down at his plate, he was watching my hands, folded in front of me. I shot a glance at Bennett and he was laser focused on our table, ready to strike at the first sign of trouble. It was times like these, the military in the man was so visible. I gave him a thumbs up and kept talking.

"So anyway, we'd jump in that creek every chance we got, me and Jerome and CJ. The thing was, I could never let my momma find out. She would paddle me seven ways to Sunday if she knew I was wearing my nice, embroidered jumpsuits in that nasty old creek water. She'd tell me I was from Georgia, not Mississippi, and young ladies from Georgia were good and proper. They didn't go running around the woods with dirty old boys and they certainly didn't swim in muddy creeks."

"I know that's what she'd say, because one day, Jerome's momma—an accomplice when it came to our secret creek visits—had to go to town on a last-minute errand and wasn't there to wash my jumper when I snuck in the back door looking like a drowned cat. And let me tell you, all hell broke loose that day. But, do you think that stopped us?"

"No?" Raf spoke, raising his head and looking me dead in the eye. And Bennett, bless his heart, was just in time to witness it.

"You're right. It didn't. But because of that day, I learned how to use the washing machine. Then Nanny B (that's what we called Jerome's momma) would make me wash my own muddy creek clothes."

"You… go… home…?" His words hardly even qualified as a murmur, but by God, I was going to find out what he was saying.

"I'm sorry Raf, I couldn't hear you. Could you repeat that?"

He cleared his throat and tried again. "Do you go home and swim still? With your boys?" I smiled as I tried to swallow the myriad of emotions welling up inside of me. Of all the things in all the world I could possibly be talking about—with what clearly was a homeless man—this was not a topic I expected to land on.

"No, Raf, I can't do that anymore." I tried to telepathically apologize to Bennett for what was about to come out of my mouth, because I refused to lie to the broken man in front of me. "You see, Jerome and CJ both went to Iraq to fight in Operation Desert

Shield and, well, only one of them came back." A hot tear slipped down my cheek, mirroring the one falling down Raf's face.

"RJ?" He asked, as hope bloomed in his eyes.

"No, my friend was CJ. He never even told me what the letters stood for, or I'd tell you. He died over there." I swiped under my eyes, drying my face in the process. "But Jerome came back. He was a medic and he did great work over there."

"Did he know RJ?" Questions swam around in my head as I wondered how to handle the predicament I had no one to blame for but myself. Raf's eyes held the innocence of a child and I wished that I could say something to ease his troubled mind and wounded soul.

"You know what, I'm not sure if Jerome ever got to meet RJ or not, but if he had, I'm sure he would tell us your son was strong and brave and a true hero. Because that's what I think about RJ and that's what I think about you, too, Raf." My eyes sought out Bennett's. *Yes? Did I do okay?* I used every facial expression I knew to seek approval, but as it turned out, I didn't need it.

"You are brave and strong, Jillian. Just like RJ." A smile graced Raf's face as he spoke.

"Thank you, Raf." He handed me his napkin, which I gladly took, before he hunkered down and finished his dinner. Only when he stood to leave did I notice that Raf only had one hand.

"That, Princess Jillian, was amazing." I preened at his compliment. Once Raf was gone, we'd jumped in to help the understaffed volunteer group, which put me serving and keeping the ice machine full, and Bennett in the kitchen trying to tackle the mountain of dishes before it started spilling out the back door. At some point, a soda spigot grew a mind of its own, soaking me from chest to knees. But Bennett swooped in, replacing my sodden apron with his own, ever the gentleman. It was nice when we finally met up again in the dining room, exhausted but alive, after the events of the night.

"I was worried about mentioning the war, but I didn't want to lie to him." And it was true. The man had given not only his sanity, but his son for the country. The least we could do for him is tell him the truth.

"I think your honesty was a refreshing change from what he's used to. He was more engaged with you than I've ever seen him. The only way I know his backstory is from the lady at the shelter, who got the information from his sister when she came looking for him."

"Wait, he has a sister and he's living in a homeless shelter?" I'd been searching through my purse for my keys, but his declaration got my attention and sent my blood boiling.

"Calm down, Princess." He placed a hand on my

shoulder and I wondered if he knew my heart did funny things when he touched me. "He stays at the shelter by choice. His sister isn't in any shape to care for him and, though she would, he's levelheaded enough to recognize that. Plus, he has an arrangement with the shelter. He has his own room, which is really more of a closet, but in exchange he cleans and fixes things around the place. It's really a win-win for everyone."

"Well, no wonder he's depressed. He's not a whole person anymore. I mean, how does he clean and fix things with only one hand? My daddy used to make jokes about my brother being as useful as a one-armed wallpaper hanger, but only in close company. This is the first time I've ever actually put an image to the saying."

When I felt my face scrunching up picturing the stump where his hand used to be, I schooled my features, but Bennett saw right through me. The corners of his mouth turned down and his whiskey-colored eyes lost some of their spark. For some reason, the idea of Bennett being disappointed in me sat in my gut like a concrete block.

"Oh, Princess. You'd be surprised what the human body can be trained to do, to compensate for a devastating loss."

I left Bennett with acid bubbling in my stomach. A melancholy surrounded us like a dense fog as we said our goodbyes and I scurried to my car. I couldn't even listen to the radio on my way home; my mind was so absorbed in all that had taken place and how the tone of the evening had shifted so rapidly and without warning. What had I done? Maybe I'd said something wrong? But he'd been offended, of *that* there was no doubt. And I was responsible for it.

As if I'd sprinted the entire way home, I was exhausted and spent when I reached the condo. Unlocking the door, I threw my keys on the table in the foyer and contemplated going straight up to bed, if for no other reason than to be done with this day already. But the blinking red light on the answering machine would have haunted my dreams.

"Jillian, darling, this is your mother. Just making sure we're all set for Thanksgiving next week. Gareth will be flying into Austin-Bergstrom Wednesday evening and your father and I think it best for you to be the one to greet him. I wouldn't be surprised if members of the media were there, too. Call back today dear. Goodbye."

I hit erase and headed for the shower, ignoring her request. I was getting so damn sick of what my father and she thought *was best*. I was an adult, and yet, they still controlled everything. *They* controlled the direction of my life, *they* held the compass. They'd predetermined years ago the world in which I'd be a part of, but at what cost to me? As I lifted the sweatshirt off my body, I was overwhelmed with the piney scent my mind connected to the hunky soldier I'd spent the evening with. And for the first time, I started to question the decisions made for me over the last decade. My parents had my life all mapped out, but maybe it was the wrong map. Maybe I needed to take control of my journey.

Chapter 15

Bennett

AT THE BEGINNING of the semester, I'd been given the name of a grad student named Paul. Part of his dissertation included behavioral therapy, specializing in the emotional health of combat veterans. And I guess because of my work in Germany (which I'd spoken of a time or two in class), my psych professor put us in contact. I agreed to be a case study. What I was really agreeing to was a series of interviews over the course of the semester.

Paul was a rather drab fellow: a tall, thin stick of a man, dressed in neatly pressed grey slacks, a starched white button-down shirt, and a navy blue sweater-vest. His vest hid all but the top of a maroon tie, modeling a perfect Windsor knot. His thin, black leather belt matched his wing tips to perfection. I'd concocted an image of what a psychology PhD student would look like and my imagination did not disappoint. I assumed our first meeting would be of the basic *get to know you* variety. So on that day, I hadn't prepared myself to spill it all just yet.

"*Sergeant Hanson, it's a pleasure to meet you. I greatly appreciate your willingness to participate in this study and I thank you for your service.*" While I'd been expecting the young Mr. Rogers look, I had not been expecting the British accent. I took his hand and loosened my grasp when I saw him wince. He was a lacy Brit from the looks of it.

"*Why are you thanking me? My service was for my country, not yours.*" 'Thank you for your service' carried no weight. It was a filler that really said, 'I have no idea what to say to someone who literally killed people, while I was taking warm showers and eating real meat.' From my limited experience with civvies since coming back, I've learned that people have no idea how to talk to a newly returned soldier. And I understood completely. When I returned, I felt like an outcast, isolated even. I'd suddenly become inconsequential and talking to noncombatants was awkward and laborious. The deficit in life experience was just too great. There was no common ground to be had, so why force it?

"*No. Clearly, I wasn't born here. I'm from Wales, but I married a Texan and by default, doesn't that make me one too?*" I laughed and shook my head, because no. That wasn't how it worked.

"*Being from Wales, you should understand Texans better than anyone. Like y'all, we believe Texas is our own country and far superior to the rest of the people that pledge allegiance to the red, white, and blue. Show me someone with the Indiana flag tattooed on their arm, for example, and I may consider your argument.*" I raised the sleeve of my T-shirt to show him the Republic of Texas flag on the bicep of my right *arm. There was a matching American flag on the left, but the Texas flag was bigger. Because everything was bigger in Texas.*

"Duly noted."

"Why don't we talk about you first?" I sat back. I was a beast at turning the tables. I was famous for getting my teachers off track in high school. A legend.

"I'm from Wales, as you know. Studied at Oxford before coming to the States to get my master's degree at NYU. In New York, I met a pretty little tourist on holiday with her parents and the rest is history. I came to Texas and married that girl before she realized she was loads above my station and we landed here. She's in grad school. Dairy science." I blanched and so did he. Apparently we both felt the same way about her particular choice of study. But hey, to each his own. "Anyway, I'm specializing in cognitive behavioral therapy and eventually plan to help people work through grief, post-traumatic stress disorder, and the like."

"So, Sergeant, why is it when I chose the psychological well-being of postwar soldiers as my topic of study, Dr. Dean mentioned your name first and without hesitation?"

"Well, I'm a postwar soldier so… " I raised my eyebrows. I was being an ass and I was fully aware of it. But, bullets and bombs were a picnic in the park compared to the invisible shit that attacked my mind. As a kid, I was never scared of monsters under the bed. As an adult, I learned they aren't under the bed. They're inside of me.

"Dr. Dean has spoken of your bravery." He just let the statement hang there in the air, like humidity or fog.

"Bravery is strangely subjective, Paul." Because yeah, sure, I could face death and stare into the eyes of my enemy, but I was powerless against myself. I was starting to appreciate the emotionless safe place the army provided and missed the safety of combat.

"And do you sleep at night, Sergeant Hanson?" I threw my head back and stared at the ceiling. Thirty-six. That's how many insulated tiles were up there, forming a perfect grid. I counted them three times before I responded.

"Falling asleep is easy."

"But you don't stay asleep, do you?" I shook my head. "Have you spoken to anyone about that day, Sergeant?" Another shake of my head.

"No one." Because the only person I could ever talk to about that had been turned into ash, put in a box, and shipped to New York... leaving me behind in Germany with invisible wounds deeper than any effect the bomb had on my body.

"Maybe that's where we need to start."

"About damn time." I muttered under my breath, taking one last drag on my cig, before stomping it out in the packed sand.

Chance was coming through, yelling "Make a hole!" as

the convoy commander followed him like a puppy. I'd been on standby for well over an hour after being voluntold to lead the convoy to Doha. I swear I'd walked around the truck, checking tires at least ten times out of sheer boredom.

"What the shit took so long?"

Chance just shrugged, that big cheesy smile of his making his eyes all but disappear. "Embrace the suck, my friend. Hurry up and wait is the name of the game these days." He threw me my bucket before putting his on. "Cover your grape, man. You can't take another hit." That made me laugh. He was the one with two concussions under his belt since we'd been out here. If anyone couldn't take a hit, it wasn't me.

"Here man, you drive." I tossed the keys and climbed in, riding shotgun. It took a few minutes to gather the troops, but soon we were on the road. Chance and I were providing security for trucks picking up things like mail, water, food, and parts.

It was a nasty ride. I'd woken up that morning with this churning in my gut, but I assumed the canned sausages, also known as the 'five fingers of death,' I'd eaten before bed had been the culprit. So I popped some Tums and went about my day. It returned in full force when we came upon a concrete Jersey barrier blocking our usual route. Chance stopped and we locked eyes. Nothing about this was right and danger hung in the air right alongside the unasked question—Do we or don't we? We both nodded at the same time.

Grabbing the radio, I called, "Oscar Mike." On the move, letting the convoy know we were pushing forward.

"Licky chicky" crackled back. Loud and clear. Chance hooked a left, taking a well-known, but often avoided alternate route. The new path took us through very fine sand, which reduced visibility. I sat up straighter in my seat and became acutely aware of my heart, bounding around in my ribcage.

As we pulled into the small village this unexpected detour ran through, my subconscious screamed at me to turn back. Where were the children that were usually out playing with a tattered ball or sword fighting with sticks in the streets? Where were the women hanging clothes on the line? A dog rambled out from behind a squally outbuilding and I jumped. My senses were functioning in hyper vigilant mode. I felt like Superman: eyes wide open, always watching, smelling, feeling, tasting.

Out here in the desert, the sand settles on everything, casting a warm tone, like looking through a sepia lens. The sun even blew out the sky, letting homesickness settle deep within my soul. I'd give anything for the smell of rain or a sky full of Bob Ross's happy clouds. I missed the color green.

When we reached the outskirts, safe, we both breathed a collective sigh of relief. Chance grabbed the picture from his shirt pocket over his heart and kissed it. I'm not even sure he knew what he'd done.

"Just expected Ali Baba to come flyin' in any minute." I nodded.

The road outside the village kicked up so much dust we were forced to mask our noses and mouths with a bandana. It was fairly ineffective and made it feel ten degrees hotter than hell, but it was something to focus on.

"CP a hundred yards northeast." Chance scoured the right, while I kept eyes on the left. This checkpoint was new. And anything new in the desert was automatically considered hazardous until we knew otherwise. We were moving into dangerous territory and for a moment, I wondered if I'd wake up tomorrow.

Chance radioed back, but as we rolled up, it was plain to see the CP was devoid of life. Where was everyone? Ten yards ahead was another Jersey barrier. Chance radioed that intel back, but we were ordered to go around. It was a risky move, but one thing you learn early on is to do as you're told.

They say the number of seconds between thunder and lightning can determine how far away the storm is. The blinding came first, followed by a blast I felt in the roots of my teeth. Then the Humvee launched into the air.

"What happened next?" I was lost in the past, but his words pulled me out. I could have cried, I was that grateful.

"I only remember bits and pieces after that. They come to me in dreams so real I can smell the tinny scent of blood."

"The human mind has a tendency to blur the lines between dreams and reality." Really? You think? It took three schools on two continents and probably close to a hundred grand to conceive that little nugget of information? Paul wrote, the scratch of his pencil echoing through the stale room. Make all *the notes you want, bud. It won't make you an expert on me. You weren't there.*

But I told him what I could. Night terrors usually involved my buddy Chance or other members of my squad and usually contained elements of the day our convoy was attacked. They were disturbing, frequent, and often very graphic. And, truly, I was ready to have them gone.

"Mr. Hanson, do you keep a journal?" Paul's face was quizzical, as if he honestly expected there to be any answer other than, 'I'm a man, so hell no.'

I cleared my throat and tried to keep a straight face. "Uh, no Paul. No uterus, no journal." His smile was tight as he wrote my revelation onto his yellow legal pad.

"I'd like you to start. We need to track how frequently these terrors are occurring and see if there's a pattern. Just make a quick note of your activities each day, bullet points even. And the next morning, note if the night terrors occurred and, if possible, the nature of the dream."

I nodded, defeated. I could do that.

And I did. For eight weeks, I cataloged my daily happenings and made note of terrors. I was even able to sketch or describe details of the dreams on a handful of occasions. And I'd never admit it, but writing about things helped. It kept me grounded, in the moment, something I sorely needed.

Paul and I met on the third floor of the library, in

a study carrel he'd reserved specifically for our interviews. Privacy was of utmost importance to Paul and the man took his job very seriously, which I appreciated. He'd taken the journal a few days prior and we were meeting to discuss it, or something. I couldn't imagine how *wake up, eat breakfast, go to class, eat lunch, go to class, study, study, study, sleep, rinse and repeat* was going to tell him anything, but I arrived at the meeting open-minded.

"So, Bennett. How've you been?" We shook hands, as per our routine.

"Same ole, same ole. Same as I've been telling you for the last few months." I shrugged as I took a seat in my usual chair.

"Well, not according to this. Your journal indicates the nightmares have eased off. Look at this." Paul placed a graph in front of me.

"What am I looking at, exactly?" I was a little embarrassed, but the red line, jagged with peaks and valleys, was like reading a foreign language.

"Look here." He pointed to the left of the page. "When you first started journaling, the terrors came every night, sometimes two or three times if you were ever able to fall asleep again. But after a few weeks of that, they lessened. By a few weeks later, the frequency dropped even more. It looks like now, you're only having one, maybe two a week."

As Paul spoke, the crooked line started to gain meaning. The dreams *had* decreased significantly, and I realized, for the first time in almost two years, I was sleeping at night.

"I found something that may also be of interest to you. Look at this." It was a bar graph this time, with the days of the week running along the bottom. "In entering the data for my study, I noticed the majority of your terrors come Sunday through Tuesday nights. You almost never have one on a Wednesday, Thursday, or Friday night. And very seldom do we see them occur on a Saturday night."

"Huh." I mumbled, staring at the document.

"Yes, so I dug a little deeper." Paul was almost giddy as he flipped through my journal. "And I noticed a correlation between your volunteer work and the decreased dream activity." *Interesting, indeed.*

My brows shot up and I looked up to meet Paul's eyes. He was staring at me, trying to read my body language, and seemed satisfied at catching me off guard.

He continued to watch carefully as I flipped back and forth between the two documents. When I could no longer take it, I looked up at him. "What?"

"I'm curious as to what happens on Wednesday and Friday nights that gives you such peace."

I'm thinking it's not a 'what,' but more like a 'who.'

My thoughts were on a Tilt-A-Whirl, but I just shrugged my shoulders and smiled, checking my watch, thinking how I would be face-to-face with the anonymous topic of our discussion in just a little over an hour.

Leaving the library through the front doors, I was headed to the cafe a little early when I ran into Chance.

"No cafe today, my friend. A water main busted a few blocks over and the water will be cut for the next few hours."

Relief suffused my soul and I viewed the water main break as a reprieve. A bullet dodged. A stay of execution.

Because, I was in no way prepared for the Pandora's box that good old Paul may have just accidentally opened and I was in desperate need of time to process it all.

Chapter 16

Jillian

THIS WAS IT—the finale. The last dinner before we settled the bet. I figured he'd pull out all the stops for this one. But after the previous three, nothing short of a destitute, homeless orphan could tug on my heartstrings any harder.

"Today's dinner is going to be a little different." Bennett met me at the doors of the cafe, both of us having walked from campus, from opposite directions.

"Different good? Or different bad? The last time you used that word, I ended up eating dinner with an amputee army vet."

"And was that so bad?" His head was tilted, awaiting my reply.

"Not at all. It was actually therapeutic in a way." And it had been.

"Good to know. Now, follow me." So I did… through the front doors and right out the back. A basket of food was waiting for us on a picnic table that, had it been a building, would have been condemned years ago. 'Rustic' is the term used when something's old, but people still want to keep it around. So, I guess the old, rickety table was about as *rustic* as possible.

The wind blew and I was thankful I'd come prepared for the crisp bite in the air, with khaki riding pants, a thick oversized denim button-down, and knee-high leather boots. Fall in Texas could be eighty degrees one day and forty degrees the next.

"Dig in." We'd both taken a seat and, thank God for small favors, the table held up under our weight.

"No, I'm waiting for our guest." Poor or not, the person deserved the common courtesy of waiting until he or she arrived. But Bennett shook his head, a knowing grin painted on his face.

"Nope... tonight, I'm your guest." I looked around, hoping he was joking, but we were alone.

Wait, was this a date? Surely this wasn't a date! I took him in through a different lens; dark-washed Levi's, black thermal shirt, heavy beige Carhartt jacket, and his usual black combat boots. Nope, same old Bennett, ruggedly casual with his *I don't care* hair. It was definitely *not* a date.

"And before you ask, no, this is not a date." My jaw dropped. *God, how'd he do that?* "Do you remember back to the first barbecue night?"

"Yeah, the night we met. That was the night you changed my tire." *And my life.*

Wait, what?

"Right. Well, that night I was a *guest*. I was here to eat, because I needed food and didn't have much." His voice was bold and self-assured. And while I never wanted to believe that was the case, his revelation wasn't a complete shock. "Do you want to know more?" I nodded. "Okay, ask away."

"Where are you from? Where did you grow up?"

"Those are two very different questions. I'm from East Texas. I guess you could say my parents were in 'sales.' They dealt drugs from our living room." I couldn't rein in the gasp. "When I was in middle school, they were both arrested and sent away for a very long time, which left me with no guardians."

"So, then what?" I was intrigued.

"So, I bounced around in the system a little, the typical 'made for TV' movie plotline, then I landed on a ranch for foster kids."

"Wait. Those exist?" I was fascinated. Bennett nodded.

"Most of the kids were troubled, unadoptable. That wasn't exactly the case for me, though. I wasn't too much trouble and I was, in fact, eligible to be adopted, but no one really wants to adopt a kid with more facial hair by 5:00 than they can grow in three days."

The sun had started to set and the wind picked up, leaves swirling at our feet. I longed for my wool pea coat, which was still sitting in the passenger seat of my car. As if my thoughts were flashing on a neon sign above my head, Bennett placed his jacket over my shoulders. And, of course, as with anything in the proximity of Bennett Hanson, the scent of an evergreen forest in winter came with it.

"So what happened?"

"Well, I was kinda stuck there for a few years until I aged out."

Oh, my heart.

"Was it awful? Were you safe?" My tone revealed more emotion than I was ready to admit. I could just picture Bennett, a sweet boy with no parents, just trying to find his place in this big world. I ached for the child he had been.

"No, it wasn't bad at all. I ended up living with a wonderful couple, Rosie and Doc, on a 600-acre ranch a little northwest of here. Rosie was a true Mexican mama in every sense of the word. She hovered, she worried, she fussed, she filled me with good food, and slapped me good when I gave her grief. She was exactly what I needed. Doc was different though. He believed in, '*Walk softly and carry a big stick.*' Kids would be placed at the ranch after being kicked out of home after home, thinking they could run all over Doc. But I saw him set an egocentric little jackass straight a time or two and knew right away I wanted no part of Doc's bad side."

"He sounds incredibly intimidating, and terrifying," I mused. My parents had never been home. As long as I followed Nanny B's rules, I was fine. And that was easy. She loved me like her own.

"Yep. Exactly what I needed. But then I turned eighteen, and I had to figure something out."

Chapter 17

Bennett

"WHY? If Rosie and Doc were so great, why didn't they let you stay?" I smiled, thinking back to those late night conversations with Doc as we mucked stalls or fixed loose boards. There was so much to be done on the ranch and there just weren't enough hours in the day.

"I could have stayed. In fact, Doc did all but beg me to stay on and work with the boys. I was good with them. They saw me as a peer and were more comfortable opening up to me. I thought about staying, but there was a whole, big world out there and I wanted to conquer it."

"And did you?" It seemed apparent that I hadn't, seeing as how this entire conversation stemmed from my needing free food, but I saw it a different way.

"Well, I did my damndest. I joined the United States Army. After basic, I spent a few weeks in Panama, nothing major. But then, the disturbance in the Gulf came about and it was no longer fun and games. Mine was one of the first troops on the ground over there and all of the sudden, I was playing with the big boys."

"Did you see a lot of action?" *If she only knew.*

"More than I cared to, that's for sure. When the battle finally came, we weren't prepared... or at least not like I thought we would be. But you can't dress rehearse a tragedy like that. My last day in battle, I lost my best buddy. We did everything together and, at least in the army, I didn't know how to be me without him. That was probably the hardest thing I've ever had to go through." Jillian's eyes clouded over and I worried that she was thinking of the friend she lost. I hated to be the cause of her pain.

"But now, you're here. How did that happen?"

"Well, after a delay in Germany, I made it back to the States and long story short, with nothing holding me back, I decided to give college a try."

"So, I'm confused. Didn't you earn paychecks for serving?" I nodded. "How old are you?"

"I'm twenty-two."

"Okay." Her eyes rolled up as she mentally crunched the numbers. "So for roughly four years, you collected a paycheck, yeah? If you were active duty that whole time, then you had basically no expenses. Seems to me you'd have more than enough for a hot meal now, right?"

"But, things aren't always as they seem, as you've

learned. You see, the ranch where Rosie and Doc lived was owned by an older gentleman and when he died, leaving no will, it became property of the state. But, the state had no use for an average plot of land in North Texas, so the whole ranch went up for auction."

"So, what? What happened?" Our food hadn't even been touched. Jillian was hanging on my every word.

"I bought the ranch, or at least half of it. Doc and Rosie were able to secure a loan for the other half."

"So, you spent your *entire* life savings to save a ranch for people you'd only known a few years?"

"No, I invested my entire savings to save the ranch that saved me. And if that ranch saves one more child, or a thousand, it will have been worth every penny." Phew. How I got through all of that without my eyeballs sweating, I will never know.

"So, where do you live now?" And there it was, the one question I absolutely had to lie about. Jillian started to unpack our dinner and I thanked the Lord above for the distraction of food.

"I have a small apartment in a building within walking distance of all my classes." There. Not a lie. Not really.

Dinner was delicious. In an insulated warming pot, we found thick beef stew with big chunks of red potatoes, carrots, and onions. Steam poured out as soon as I removed the lid and seconds later, Jillian was warming her hands on a bowlful while I shoveled it into my mouth like someone was about to steal it away.

"Hungry, were ya?" she teased and I nodded, mouth too full to answer. She laughed. "Here, save room for these." Jillian reached into the basket and pulled out a plastic wrap-covered plate, containing two of the most enormous brownies I'd ever seen.

"Don't worry, I'll have room." And for a second, just one second, I saw a flash of pity in her eyes, reminding me of who I was. *The Princess and the Pauper*, or *Soldier*, if I had to put an accurate label on it.

In the end, Jillian gave me her brownie too, something about needing to fit into a dress, or something. With the remnants of what proved to be one of the best meals I'd had in months packed back into the basket, we returned to the kitchen.

"How was everything?" Mrs. Lowe was just finishing the night's dishes. The cafe menu had been chicken noodle soup and grilled cheese, so I knew either she or Chance had made this meal specifically for us.

"Perfect. Absolutely perfect." Jillian replied with a satisfied sigh, placing her hand over her nonexistent stomach. Lillie Lowe beamed at her sincere words and I nodded in agreement.

"I'm stuffed." I rubbed my pooched-out belly for effect, making Jillian laugh for the second time that night. It scared me, how proud I was to have made her happy. I needed to get a rein on whatever the hell this was going on inside of me.

Having everything under control at the cafe, Lillie shooed us off and I agreed to let Jillian drop me off at the library, as she had several times before. Pulling up to the curb, my usual drop-off point, she put the car in park.

This is new.

"Thank you for sharing your story." Her words were soft, sincere.

"You're welcome." Mine mirrored hers. She sucked in a deep breath, letting it out slowly through puckered lips, a good indicator she had something on her mind.

In the army, I'd learned that a person's words are only one communication tool, and a very unreliable one at that. Sure, hear the words, but watch the face, observe the body. That's usually where the truth would shine through, often trumping the actual words to a degree. But all traces of light were gone, leaving in its wake a cloud-filled, inky sky. I could scarcely make out her features, thanks to the fluorescent lights on the street. And it was not enough to get a read on her.

"You win." *Sorry, what was that again?*

"What?"

"The bet. You win the bet." Her breaths were coming quick, shallow, and almost as if she, herself, couldn't believe what she was saying. *The bet.* I'd almost forgotten about the bet, so busy just enjoying being with her. It must have taken a lot to admit that and she certainly didn't have to. She could have lied. How would I have known?

"So, you'll help with Thanksgiving?" *I needed to tone down the excitement.*

I knew she had a family. Wouldn't they miss her? When I initiated this ridiculous bet, I was one hundred percent certain I would lose.

"Yep." Her small smile was endearing, making my heart flutter like a caged bird. I squeezed my eyes shut, to clear my mind.

"Okay. From what Chance explained to me the other night, the Lowes start on Wednesday night with the prep and meet the volunteers back up there around 9:00 Thanksgiving morning. Dinner is served at 6:00."

She nodded, and I grabbed the door handle to get out, then changed my mind. "Your whole day will be spent at the cafe. There won't be time for you to go be with your family." I paused, willing some night vision superpower to kick in so I could see her expression. I opened the door, just enough to make the dome light come on. She blinked several times, allowing her pupils to contract accordingly. "Are you sure you want to do this?"

Her face said nothing, but her steely eyes had water

collecting in the corners. *Was it from the cold, or something else?* Cocking her head to one side, she nodded slowly, almost imperceptible. "More than anything else in the world."

The Community Cafe was closed the Wednesday before Thanksgiving to allow the volunteers to prepare for the flood of bodies that were expected to come through the doors the following evening. Lillie and Chance said they fed about three times their usual crowd each year and assured us that, if done properly, this meal would run just as smoothly as the rest of them. That remained to be seen.

After class, I headed straight for the cafe and my heart jumped when a shiny blue BMW, parked in its usual space, came into view.

Stop.

I had to stop. This, whatever it was, needed to be extinguished. I was setting myself up for nothing but misery, letting these feelings grow. Shaking the thought from my head, I hurried in, out of the cold.

The cafe felt alive, a cacophony of clatters and laughter creating a vortex of warmth and comfort. And for the first time in a long time, I didn't miss the camaraderie of the army. I was finally finding my place and there was much to be thankful for this year.

"Howdy." I poked my head into the kitchen

before putting my backpack in the office and grabbing an apron.

I waved to a few people I recognized from the library, setting up portable tables and chairs in the dining room. A few more were filling salt and pepper shakers. Sports Talk was blaring on the radio.

Lillie was washing vegetables at the small sink, then handing them over to Chance, whose cutting and chopping technique was more like a dance than a mundane task. The man was from New Orleans and master of his kitchen.

"Where do you want me?" I asked, walking around to assess all the different preparation areas. Jillian was radiant. Her blonde hair was swept up in a loose bun, showing off her long neck, and those jeans… they deserved a standing ovation for how well they molded to her body.

She'd been running water at the sink since I walked in the door and then turned toward the stove, carrying a large stockpot of water just as I was passing behind her. All at once and in slow motion, her boot caught on my retreating leg, causing water to splash all over the floor and soaking my right leg. I looked like I'd stepped in a lake.

I watched the pot clatter to the tile, trying to come up with a witty comment, but when I looked back up and saw her face, I stopped.

"What?" My heart pounded. Clearly, I'd missed something. Jillian stood still as death, eyes wide, taking me in as if I were the Grim Reaper.

"Jillian, *what?* " I stepped over the pot, backtracking to reach her, but she shook her head, pointing to the wet leg of my jeans. "It's no big deal, Princess. I'll dry."

Lillie continued her chopping, used to commotion in the kitchen, but Jillian looked as if she'd been dipped in starch. I moved toward her, slowly, so as not to spook her further. But for the life of me, I couldn't figure out what was going on with her. When I was standing right in front of her she looked up into my eyes and whispered, "Bennett, that water was near boiling."

I looked down and saw steam rising from the puddle at our feet. She'd been using the hot water spigot. I looked at the stove where a large bowl of diced potatoes sat, ready for boiling.

"Oh, that?" My mouth was the Sahara, but I backed up, waving her off. "Don't worry about that... high pain tolerance." I backed up some more.

She shook her head, eyes still wide as saucers. "But... you must be burned! There'll be blisters and—" She knelt down to reach for my leg.

"Stop."

I hadn't intended to spit the word at her like gunfire. "I'm... fine. Just drop it." I continued my tour of the kitchen, in search of a task. Jillian, moving with none of the confidence and superiority I'd grown to expect from her, mopped up the water, never once looking up from her task. Wringing it out, she mopped again and then maybe even a third time. When she finally finished, she flung the mop into the bucket and shoved it into the utility closet, before filling up a new pot with steaming hot water.

With salad cut, eggs boiled, cornbread baked, and vegetables sautéed, we locked up and said our goodbyes to the other volunteers. I'd automatically migrated to the passenger side of Jillian's car, but stopped with my hand on the door handle, brows raised in question. She hadn't said much since the hot water incident, so it probably wasn't wise to assume things would magically go back to normal once we left the cafe. But a faint nod, lacking eye contact, answered my unspoken question.

I'd done this. I was the reason she was hurt or mad or whatever emotion it was that stole her confidence and energy. And I hated myself for it.

"Jillian…" I whispered.

She shook her head, staring straight ahead, her hands firmly planted on ten and two. We'd already pulled up to the library, the five-minute drive shrouded in enough tension to choke an elephant. Everything in me screamed there was more to her stonewalling act, but that's not what this conversation was about.

"I snapped at you tonight. It was out of line and out of character for the man I am striving to be."

I was getting nowhere. She hadn't so much as taken a breath, so I turned in the seat to face her. "Look, when I screw up and do something I know I shouldn't have, I feel it, like physical pain. I pride myself on character and, if you don't let me get this out, it will eat me alive." She loosened her grip on the wheel and turned toward me, but kept her gaze down, still never making eye contact. In that moment, I realized her self assuredness was one of her best qualities.

Her hands were folded in her lap, so I reached out and put a hand on her arm. "I'm sorry about the way I treated you and it will never, ever happen again. You have my word and it's stronger than titanium." She nodded, which caused a tear to fall into her lap.

And... It. Broke. Me.

Without a second thought, I leaned over the console and pulled Jillian Walker into my arms, feeling her hot tears on my neck. At first, she remained stock-still, but I felt the exact moment her will dissolved. Her body melted into mine and it was the first time in so very long that I felt complete and like the person I used to be.

It couldn't have lasted more than thirty seconds. I loosened my grip, letting her go, even though everything inside of me screamed to keep her right there by my heart. As I opened the door, she swiped a hand over her face and resumed proper driving posture.

The moment my foot hit the pavement, I knew I'd made an enormous mistake. So I rushed around the front of her car and stopped beside her window. She turned her head and stared at me a moment before rolling down her window.

"Jillian?"

"Bennett?" She matched my tone precisely. I was getting my Jillian back, though I don't remember when I'd started thinking of her as mine.

Now or never.

I leaned into her window. She gasped when she realized what was happening, but centimeters from her lips, I stopped. I hadn't thought this through. What was I trying to accomplish anyw—

Her lips, feather-soft, grazed across mine. Her hands, cold and tiny and smooth, cupped my cheeks and pulled me in closer. The temperature was no more than forty degrees, yet I was lit up inside like a campfire.

I pulled away, resting my forehead against hers, feeding my breath into her lungs, as if we needed each other to survive. It was too much—it was all too much—so I backed my way out and stood up, having no clue what to say now because everything inside of me that had broken with her tears, was healed by her kiss.

"So, I'll see you tomorrow, right? Do you still want to come?"

Her head popped around and she caught my eyes for the first time in what felt like forever. With a deep, shuddering breath, she glanced down at her lap and whispered, "More than anything else in the world."

Chapter 18

Jillian

MY MOTHER ALWAYS said, *A good night's sleep is like duct tape—it can fix almost anything.* I laugh when I think about that now, because I'd bet my hefty trust fund she's never been within ten feet of a roll of duct tape. I opened my eyes to soft blue light sneaking in through the slats of my plantation blinds.

My body begged for more sleep, but my mind refused. So up I sat, covers falling around my waist as I stretched and checked the time: six in the morning. I yawned and fell back against the down pillows, still warm from where I'd just been. It was Thanksgiving Day and, due to an odd turn of events, I was to spend it with Bennett Hanson. My heart did a little flip, and I didn't even try to fight the smile that landed on my face at the thought of him.

Being around Bennett was like the thirteen-year-old me riding a roller coaster for the first time after eating a giant turkey leg, cotton candy, and a candied apple… exhilarating, yet sickening. But at the moment, exhilarating was winning. With plans to meet at nine, I had three hours and I wanted to look my best.

After my shower, I set my hair in hot curlers and applied my makeup with the utmost precision, even knowing that I'd probably end up on dish duty, where the humidity would make my face melt and my hair sag by the day's end. I didn't care, though. I felt different this morning—happier—like last night had been some sort of emotional test where Bennett was concerned and I'd passed. And been rewarded with the most precious prize. I paused, debating if I wanted to dive further into what I felt when Bennett was around, but the decision was made for me by a knock at the door.

What the hell? It was Thanksgiving. All my friends had gone home. I seriously contemplated not getting it. If ignored long enough, people tended to go away, but in the end my curiosity won out. I stomped down the stairs, throwing my robe on as I walked to the door. I jerked it open, intent on directing some poor lost soul in the right direction, but stopped short at the sight in front of me.

"Hey, beautiful." Leaning against the doorframe, with an arrogance only a man with his level of confidence could pull off, was my soon-to-be betrothed.

Gareth, with his custom-fitted, double-breasted Calvin Klein suit. Gareth, with his wavy blond hair molded into the perfect shape by what I could only assume were multiple hair products. Gareth, who, before I could even think, was reaching out, grabbing at me and tugging the sash of my robe open as he yanked my now semi-naked body flush with his. Gareth, who held on with great force when I tried to extract myself from his roaming hands and his crushing grip.

"Wh-What are you doing here?" I managed to get away, only after he pushed his way in, his swagger reminiscent of Dean Martin and the rest of the Rat Pack. It was a performance—always a performance—even without an audience. I took a moment to straighten myself out as I moved further into the condo, Gareth hot on my heels.

"Well, that's not the greeting I was expecting." He leered, his deep brown eyes drinking me in, head to toe, when a shiver ran across my skin. But not the delicious kind. The repulsed kind. There was a time in my life I would have taken immense pride in the effect my body had on a man like Gareth Johnson, but it was becoming crystal clear that time had passed.

I backed up, stopped by an antique trunk I used as a coffee table, the cool brass hinges biting into the skin at the back of my knees. Instinctively, I wrapped my arms tight across my chest, shivering, but not from the cold. Finally comprehending my defensive stance, Gareth backed off, but he wasn't happy about it. His head tilted to one side as he sized me up. A wrinkle formed between his brows, and that sharp jaw that couldn't have been more perfect had it been chiseled from stone, clenched and unclenched as the second hand on the wall clock ticked a stress-inducing rhythm.

"What the hell is wrong with you?" he spat, when the silence began to suffocate both of us.

"Me first. Why the hell are you here?" Wasn't he supposed to be at the governor's mansion, with MY parents? I'd called both my parents and him a few days ago, letting them know I had a school commitment I couldn't get out of, so he knew not to expect me. Sure, I strategically planned my calls when I was certain I'd get the answering machines and was successful on both accounts, but still. He got the message. I know he did. So what was this about?

"Surprise! I came to steal you away."

"What? Steal me away? I can't just—"

"My dad's jet is waiting at that weed-ridden concrete slab you call an airport." I was already brutally shaking my head, scooting around the trunk to put more space between us. Gareth was a large man, both in height and width, and although he never took another step, I felt like every second we stood there he got closer and closer.

"Did you think I was kidding when I said I was needed here? Did you think that was a joke?" I was yelling, but didn't really care anymore. His sneer was familiar, but it only appeared when he was trying to mask anger, or annoyance, or rage. I walked to my answering machine and listened to the one new message I'd ignored the night before.

Jillian, I think you misunderstood my invitation to celebrate Thanksgiving at the mansion. It wasn't optional. My parents are not only hosting yours, but several people that will be pivotal in my bid for the senate, so get your ass in the car and get here.

He took a deep breath and took control of his tone, lowering the volume and removing some of the venom, but that was an act. The last part of his message was the part that mattered, and I heard it loud and clear, masked by a more cheery disposition.

My dear, this is not a request and in the future, this behavior will not be tolerated. I will expect you tonight. I love you.

The message stopped. I'd been staring at the machine as if it were a third person in the room, addressing me personally. But when I looked back up to meet Gareth's eyes, the mask was gone and he was seething.

"No." One word, one syllable, yet foreign to the man in front of me.

"Excuse me?" His words were unbelieving, and dripped with disgust.

"I said '*no.*' It's this word in the English language used to signify a negative response, but you've never heard that word before, have you?" I laughed, quick and sharp, more from nerves than from the humor I didn't feel.

He was dumbfounded, mouth agape and eyes wide.

For the first time in his privileged life, someone had the balls to stand up to him.

"Jillian, these people will be arriving at the governor's mansion for cocktails in exactly," he checked his horribly gaudy Tag Heuer watch, "four hours. And when they walk through the door, the first thing they will see is their future senator, with a beautiful, smiling blonde on his arm, looking at him with adoring eyes."

And there it was. To him, I wasn't a person. I was an item, a trophy to add to his collection. He needed me, though. He knew his conservative constituents had expectations. A family man is what he needed to be, not some entitled frat boy with an inferiority complex and his daddy's American Express. They wanted a doting husband, with a pretty little wife, the house with the white picket fence, 2.5 kids, and a top-of-the-line minivan in the driveway. And the only thing standing in the way of his twisted American dream? Me.

"Gareth, get out of my way, I have somewhere to be." I pushed my way around him, heading toward my room to get dressed. I closed the door behind me, leaning up against it as I tried to wrap my brain around what had just happened. The quiet *tap tap tap* on my door prompted me to lock it.

I was disgusted and, had he not been born into Texas royalty, with people fighting at the chance to bow down at his feet, I would let him know how I really felt.

176

"Jillian?" he called softly, prompting an immediate and automatic eyeroll.

"What? I'm getting dressed." I sounded more scared than annoyed. I didn't even recognize myself anymore. It's like those people whose eyes change color depending on the color of their shirt. When they wear yellow, their eyes look green, but when they wear purple, their eyes are blue. I was the eyes... only my personality changed, depending on the man.

With Bennett, I was happy, friendly, and more relaxed than I'd been in my entire life. But with Gareth, I was this conceited, self important, uppity bitch. And that had been my way for twenty years. That was exactly what my mother bred me to be.

Tap, tap, tap.

I squeezed my eyes closed tight, wishing to be anywhere but here with him. Was I cut out for sixty more years of this man? I hadn't really ever been given the choice, but as I imagined my future, the landscape of my life began changing. No more barren land with a flat, dead end road ahead, but something different. Something I'd never had before.

Choices.

Tap, tap, tap.

I shook my head, thinking about her, my mother, and what must be rolling around in her privileged, entitled head. Because anything less than perfect was viewed as a sin in her eyes. Growing up, I was a show pony—always on display. In reality though, I was ignored. Nonexistent. Interesting how Gareth has ignored me for months, but now that he needs a show pony, he's flying a private jet into town to get me.

Tap tap tap again.

Damn it!

"Can you at least tell me where you're going?" For a minute, he sounded like my Gareth, the one I adored, no, worshipped for most of my life. But was that Gareth even real? Just as I'd been bred for the country club set, he'd been bred for politics. He was a born chameleon.

I sighed, tossed my robe to the floor, and quickly threw on my underthings and my denim wrap dress. Yanking the door open, I rushed by to slip on my cowboy boots, not because that's what I'd planned to wear, but because I was late and needed to get on the road. "I'm going to the Community Cafe." I looked at the hook beside the front door, but it was empty. I ran back to my room, checked the bathroom, then my jacket pocket with no luck. Now was not the time for my keys to play hide-and-go-seek. *Couldn't I just catch a break?*

After checking the kitchen with no luck, I turned the corner and there was Gareth. He stood by the door, tossing my keys in the air and catching them, a boyish grin plastered across his face. Another mask, I was sure of it.

"Well, I guess *we'd* better go," he sang with a wink. My mother always said, *You've got to pick your battles and you should only pick the ones you're guaranteed to win.* Holding the keys, he held all the power and it was time I admitted defeat. I stomped past him and out into the frigid air. The wind was strong, blowing my hair into my face, a few strands sticking to my lip gloss. He may have forced my hand in accompanying me to the cafe, but he wasn't going to make me like it.

"Jillian, I don't understand why you're being so difficult. Why are you even associating with people like this?" I rolled my eyes as we traveled down the road. His choice of words struck me as funny and sad at the same time. Funny, because he was so out of touch with anyone earning less than a six-figure salary… and sad because I'd heard those words before in my own head. Had I sounded like this just a few months ago? I shook my head, already knowing the answer.

"This is where I do my community service. It's in the agreement you bullied the DA into making for me. You remember, don't you? The night I caught you trying to examine Lori's tonsils with your tongue? The night you followed me from the party and chased me up a pole with your fancy new Ferrari? The night our baby died and I almost did too? Surely that fateful night hasn't slipped your mind. God knows you reminded me about it for long enough."

"It was a *fetus*, Jillian, *not a baby*. And I thought we agreed to leave the past in the past? You need to grow up. Anyway, I figured you'd work in an office or something, not play servant girl to lazy, penniless wretches."

"It's not like that, Gareth." He pretended he didn't hear me, but he did.

"Don't worry, I'll have a talk with the DA. Where's your phone?" He was already reaching into the console between the seats to pull it out.

"What? No!" *Moron.* I tried to bat it out of his hand and he nearly steered us into a ditch, before pulling into the all too familiar parking lot in front of a little, run-down building I'd grown to love. He threw the car in park and turned to face me, phone in hand, dialing while he spoke.

"Stop being such a bitch, Jillian. I'm just leaving a message for Dad to let him know we've been detained. We must take off no later than eleven or we won't make it and, well, that's not acceptable." He left a quick message with his father's personal assistant, who apparently wasn't allowed a holiday, then stuck the phone back in its hiding place.

"Alright, now let's go in there so you can get this nonsense out of your system and we can get back to being us. I've missed you, Jillian." From his lips, my name was vile. When he trailed one finger down the side of my face, the only skin visible and within his reach, a cold chill crept down my spine. I thought I might vomit. This was wrong… everything about him was wrong. Because with Gareth, I felt stunted by his stagnant disinterest in who I was as a person. I hadn't realized how vital that was to my existence until meeting Bennett and I found that utterly terrifying. Things couldn't go on the way they were, that was obvious. Gareth reached for the door handle and I screamed inside, knowing I was about to introduce a toxin into the purest part of my life.

My worst fears were confirmed when Bennett turned the corner at the exact moment Gareth unfurled his lanky body from the driver's side of my car. "I thought you said the homeless people weren't going to be here until later." I froze. Gareth was a big personality, with a big booming voice that carried. Far. I had no doubt anyone within a two-block radius heard him, as I'm sure was his goal. He was the Bobby Fischer of intimidation.

"Jillian?" Tears pricked my eyes, and by closing them I could so easily picture the little boy, whose parents had just been taken away, scared and alone, wondering where he'd lay his head that night. Bennett's voice was a mixture of curiosity, disappointment, and fear. And it was because of me. My heart cracked.

"Jillian, stop." Gareth boomed. How was it that my name from one man's mouth sounded like a song, and from another just seconds later, sounded like an expletive?

"What?" I continued to the sidewalk that lead to the cafe doors.

"No, Jillian. I said stop. Get behind me. Now." Gareth's words were clipped and harsh, more appropriate for a petulant child who was about to run into the street or touch a hot iron. Not for a grown woman. And he huffed in annoyance when I didn't immediately comply, rounding the car to do what? Physically force me to move?

That's when Bennett stepped up. "Hang on there, bud. If I know anything about this woman right here, it's that she does what she wants, when she wants. And right now, it appears she doesn't want to get behind you."

Gareth's chest started to puff out, reminding me of those bullfrogs that blew bubbles from their necks to make themselves look fierce, or a peacock preening his feathers. If he was trying to make himself look intimidating, he picked the wrong soldier to engage in a pissing contest.

Each step Gareth moved toward me, Bennett matched. Soon, I would be a Jillian sandwich, and while that would be a dream for the majority of my sorority sisters, it was becoming my worst nightmare.

"Both of you boys need to take a step back. Gareth, this is Bennett Hanson. He's a student, as well as an army vet, and he volunteers with me." Bennett offered his hand and Gareth growled as he took it with enough force to crush a can from the look of his white knuckles.

"Good to meet you Ben, I'm Gareth Johnson, Jillian's boyfriend. And thank you for your service." If Gareth's utterance of our relationship status came as a surprise to Bennett, it sure didn't show, as he shook the idiot's hand like the strong, self-assured man he was.

"Good to meet you, too. Are you two here to volunteer... together?" His once bright golden eyes flickered to mine and he was that little boy again—so full of questions, but lacking the words to ask—and the fissure deepened, threatening to split my heart in two.

"Yeah, man. Apparently Jillian needs to get in there and put in her time, but we really need to get moving. My plane is waiting at the airport to take us to our family dinner and we can't be late, right honey?" He grabbed my hand and pulled me into the crook of his arm, a place that used to bring me such comfort. Oh, what I would have given, just a few short months ago, to find myself wrapped in Gareth Johnson's long, tanned arms. But a lot can change in a few months. Now his touch felt like fire ants under my skin. What was wrong with me?

Bennett held the door open as Gareth entered first, dragging me over the threshold behind him. I did all I could, short of flashing Bennett, to get his attention... but he was having nothing to do with me. This wasn't the Bennett from last night. This wasn't the man who held me in his arms while I cried. This wasn't the man I was falling for. This was Bennett Hanson, Soldier. And I was the enemy.

We fell into a semi-normal routine in the kitchen. I manned the stove, the Lowes did food prep on the stainless steel island, and Bennett was all over the place doing whatever was asked of him. Gareth, meanwhile, sat at a table in the dining room reading the Wall Street Journal, though where he dug that up, I'll never know.

When I had accepted the fact Bennett was at a new level of pissed and was not going to acknowledge my existence in any way, shape, or form, I started telepathically sending him messages. First, I launched into a heartfelt apology for the way I treated him the night before, then I explained Gareth's sudden and unwanted appearance. After that, I poured my heart out, letting him know how good he made me feel and how I loved the person I was when I was with him. When I was done, I looked his direction, but he was staring at the wall shared between the kitchen and the dining room. If he had x-ray vision and looks could kill, Gareth would be zapped to smithereens.

"Jillian, sweetie, I need a new roll of aluminum foil. Could you run and grab it from the pantry?" Surely Mrs. Lowe was throwing me a bone, trying to give me a break from the tension that was currently a monster with three heads.

"Sure." I smiled, but my heart wasn't in it. At the sound of my voice, Bennett looked my way, meeting my eyes. Time froze. And without uttering a word, I told him I was sorry with every fiber of my being. He told me he was sorry, too.

The aluminum foil was on the top shelf. It always had been. And I was five foot four on a good day, so even with the aid of the stainless steel step stool that hung neatly on the inside of the pantry door, there was no way I was getting that roll of tinfoil on my own.

"Bennett, be a dear and go help her. I forgot how high up it is." I heard her request from where I stood, trying to decide whether or not to climb the shelf when Bennett shuffled in. The pantry was just that—a pantry. Add two people to the collection of supplies it took to run the cafe, and it became a sardine can. But even knowing this, I didn't move to allow him room when Bennett cleared his throat. I just stood right in his path and looked at him with a wide stance, a set jaw, and loads of fake confidence. I was trying to say, *If you want me to move, you'll have to do it yourself.*

It didn't work. The man was like a mouse, contorting around me, able to fit into a space no bigger than a coffin. It was impressive.

"How's the leg?"

"Same as it was yesterday. Fine." He stood on his toes and stretched his arm high, causing his deep green thermal to rise up, showing the well-toned muscles in his back. "You're in my way."

"Bennett, why won't you talk to me?" *Stand your ground, Jill, stand your ground.*

"I'm talking to you now." His air of disinterest caused physical pain in my chest and I wanted to bang my head into the metal shelves that surrounded us. Men were impossible. I threw my arms up. Or, I tried to, but in the process, I hit the back of my left hand on an industrial-sized can of green beans, so I dropped them to my side in defeat. Bennett, by that point, had stopped trying to get the foil, probably figuring out that the task was just a ploy by the Lowes to force us together. It had to be uncomfortable for them, being right smack in the middle of our unspoken emotional crossfire.

"Fine. I'll talk. Since when do you have a boyfriend? And since when is said boyfriend the governor's son? How did I spend the entire last month with you—working together, sharing meals, sharing my life with you—without this coming up, Jillian?"

"Jill. Please."

"What?" His patience was growing thin. He wanted answers.

"Please don't call me Jillian anymore. Just Jill from now on, okay?" He nodded. "I'm sorry I never told you, it just never came up and... when I was with you, it was like he didn't exist."

He chuckled, but not the *funny, haha* kind. No, it was more like the, *quit feeding me this line of bull, spoiled rich girl who wants to have her cake and eat it too* kind. I was familiar with both.

"Well, I guess it doesn't matter at this point anyway." He checked the time on his simple watch—black with a rubber band, few dials, and even fewer features—probably purchased at Walmart for fifteen bucks. Because that's who he was. Bennett led a simple, uncomplicated life, while the place I came from was demanding and convoluted. And how I felt about him or how he didn't feel about me was of no matter. "Y'all should get on the road. And board your plane. To Austin. To the governor's mansion, is it?"

And that was the root of it all, wasn't it?

At the end of the day, we were of two different worlds and the walls separating us were too great to scale. For Bennett's sake, of that I was glad. He was out of my league. He was pure and good and drew his happiness from the happiness of others. He was hardworking, bighearted, and gave everything in life all he had. One day, he'd meet a girl and love her the same way. And in that moment, looking into his eyes, I knew without a shred of doubt that I'd give up my whole world, everything I'd ever known, to be the woman on the receiving end of his love. That was the truest truth in all of this.

I reached out and placed my hand on Bennett's jaw,

feeling the golden scruff of his beard against my skin. And for a few beats of my heart, he leaned in and closed his eyes. But love has consequences. Millions of them. And we both knew that.

We both heard Gareth's voice at the same time. He stiffened, and I yanked my hand away from the sweetest touch I'd ever known, feeling the loss like a death. Bennett backed out of the pantry and swept by as Gareth moved into the hallway.

"We've been here long enough, Jillian. Get your things and let's go." Another command, the only way he knew to communicate. I caught Bennett's eyes over Gareth's shoulder. *Say something*, I willed to him. *Say anything to keep me with you. Don't let me go. Don't let me walk away.*

But it was all for nothing. Bennett jerked his head toward the door and with a sad smile, mouthed, *Go!* That was it. The decision was made. He didn't want me and he was telling me to go back to my life, to my comfort zone with my Prince Charming. The place where I really was the *princess* he accused me of being all those months ago, when my world still revolved around me, and not him.

Gareth grabbed my hand. I didn't resist and within twenty minutes, I would be on the governor's plane, Austin bound, to face a perfectly orchestrated life I no longer wanted any part of.

We left my car in the covered parking lot and raced on to the tarmac, to the awaiting plane. From the corner of my eye, I saw people gawking at us, probably wondering who would be boarding a private jet in a small, country town on Thanksgiving. Gareth saw them too and pageant waved to his adoring fans. They probably had no idea who he was. No one on the planet thought Gareth Johnson was more important than Gareth Johnson.

"Mr. Johnson, your father—" Gareth held his hand out flat just inches from the pilot's face to halt his statement. I'd have given my eyeteeth to see the older man sucker punch him right in the jaw. He deserved it. *Arrogant asshole.*

"Davis, I am well-aware of the time and I'm sure my father will hold nothing back in letting me know his feelings on my sudden disappearance, but right now, I need you to get us in the air." Without waiting for a response, Gareth walked past the man, clanking up the steel stairs rolled out for just such an occasion, dragging me behind him.

I hated flying. Hate wasn't even a strong enough word, so when Gareth started in on me the minute the door was closed and secured, I closed my eyes and turned my head.

"Stop being a child, *Jillian.*" His words were dipped in hate and disgust. He was baiting me. A woman I hadn't noticed before gasped and I opened my eyes just in time to see her cast her wide eyes to Gareth. Her pointy little chin was trembling and she swallowed over and over again, her mouth opening in between, like she had something to say but kept forgetting. Gareth cleared his throat.

"Uhh, Jillian, this is Mallory." He swiveled in his chair to face her and with a much softer tone, said "Mallory, this is Jillian. My, um… she's… "

"The Walker girl. Yes, I know who she is, *Mister* Johnson." Cutting his eyes back to me, I raised my eyebrows, questioning him on her sudden onset of hostility. "May I get you a drink, Miss Walker?" Apparently, her anger extended to me as well.

"No thank you, Mallory. If you could just leave us, please." She lowered her head, shrinking a good three inches, then spun on the toes of her four-inch stilettos. She disappeared back into the cockpit, calling behind her that we'd be taking off shortly.

"Jesus, Jillian, did you ever think I may have needed a drink?" He ran his hand through his hair, which had been neatly combed to the side. He had the hairstyle of a five-year-old boy on Sundays. I just laughed.

"Oh, I'm surprised good ole Mallory didn't quench your thirst on the flight in." He shook his head, but his silence and the color rising from his neck to his cheeks spoke volumes. I heard the engines come to life as our speed picked up. This was the worst part. I'd rather have a root canal than fly anywhere. Unless it was

Scotland. I think I could manage that flight, knowing what was on the other side. I pinched my eyes shut and pictured the moors of Scotland, all patches of heather and peat moss. I'd been obsessed since I was small. It was my happy place, so I let imaginary bagpipe tunes drown out the confuzzled thoughts pinging around in my brain.

"I'll be right back," Gareth announced as he unbuckled his seatbelt and stood. Takeoff was uneventful and the pilot assured us it would be a smooth flight. I opened my eyes, assuming he was headed for the lavatory, but he turned the other direction.

"Really, Gareth? It's bad enough you're screwing the help, but do you have to do it when I'm right here?" I was shaking my head. He sat back down, looking like a dog caught digging up its owner's prize-winning petunias.

"Why do you even care? I certainly can't get it from you?" *Well, we were finally going to do this.* Okay.

"You did once. After plying me with Southern Comfort and Sprite. After I was so drunk I didn't know my own name. You remember that, don't you?" I was practically yelling and he was smoldering, his breaths deep and audible. I took it down a notch or ten and added, "You raped me that night, Gareth. You couldn't get what you wanted, so you just took it." I tucked my chin to my chest to gather some composure.

"It's not like I wouldn't have gotten it eventually. It was mine to take." There was no remorse in his voice, no compassion, no guilt. And the sad thing was, he probably believed the shit he was spewing. Because it *was* his, wasn't it? My father had promised him a virgin and that's exactly what he got.

"Why screw *me* when you were getting plenty from Lori and whoever else? You couldn't have waited a little longer?" The tears that had been stinging the backs of my eyes vanished, replaced with a new awareness. This man was my betrothed. He was the one whom I was supposed to promise to love and cherish and obey in a few short years. This was my future, wasn't it?

"Lori and I were just messin—"

"Is this what my life will be like with you? Am I expected to marry an off-brand Kennedy, just to be an off-brand Jackie O? You really think I'm just going to stand there and look pretty, while you sleep your way across Texas and then Washington DC?" His Adam's apple bobbed, but he didn't answer right away.

"Mr. Johnson, Ms. Walker," a deep voice said over the intercom. "We will be landing in Austin in roughly ten minutes. Please remain seated and buckle up if you aren't already."

"Jillian," he started. "You grew up with your

parents. What was their marriage like?" They were roommates at best, married in name only. "Once we're married, I honestly couldn't care less what you do, as long as you're discreet. And the sooner you pop out a kid or two, the better."

"Pop out a kid or two? Are you kidding me? Do you even listen when I talk? The steering wheel of my car punctured my uterus. It's highly unlikely I'll ever have children." I choked on that last part. It was the first time I'd said it aloud.

"Good. Then I won't have to worry about you bringing some bastard home from your dalliances." His toxic words stole the breath from my lungs and I had to take a minute to recuperate.

"And what dalliances would those be exactly?" This jerk is unbelievable.

"Like the one you're having with that blue-collar trash pretending to be your knight in shining armor this morning." *Oh my God, he is talking about Bennett.*

My breath caught in my throat as the wheels touched down on the runway. It seemed like only seconds went by and we were coming to a complete stop and men in navy blue work coveralls and orange vests were pushing a rolling stairway to the door of the plane. Gareth retrieved his attaché case from the overhead compartment and stood by the door, staring at it, as if he could make it open with the power of his mind. I may have chuckled a little as I fetched my own bag from the same overhead bin, thinking, *Bennett would have gotten my bag down first, and maybe even carried it for me.*

The second the doors opened, Gareth flew down the stairs to the awaiting town car that would, no doubt, take us both to the governor's mansion. I, however, took my time. "Goodbye, Miss Walker," Mallory chirped, regaining her cheerful composure. "I hope you had a nice flight."

I smiled, then straightened my expression and looked her straight in the eyes. "My flight was delightful, thanks so much. But I recommend you get an appointment with your lady doctor as soon as possible. Mister Johnson is coming off a bad case of the clap and he's also known to have crabs." I smiled again, and waggled my fingers at the now teary girl. "Toodle-oo. And have a happy Thanksgiving." Next thing I knew, we were flying down the highway, headed toward the heart of Austin, and with a police escort to boot.

Chapter 19

Bennett

I WAS FALLING for her. I'm not even sure how it happened or when it started, but I was definitely falling for her. I knew it the minute my lips touched hers and the stormy chaos in my mind stilled. She was my answer, she was my cure. And now she would be my undoing.

I dialed. It was late, but it needed to be done.

"Hello?" His voice was soft, gravelly even. Surely he hadn't been sleeping.

"Doc? Did I wake you?" His low, rumbly chuckle brought a little spark back to the darkness inside me.

"Naw, Rosie fell asleep on my arm while we were watching reruns of M*A*S*H and I just hate to move, you know?"

I *wish* I knew. We chatted a few minutes, about everything and nothing, but when the silence became earsplitting, he asked.

"And the girl? Rosie will kill me if I don't ask." I pulled a few deep breaths.

"How did you know, Doc? When you met Rosie, how did you know?" I realized this was something I'd have asked Chance, if he were still alive.

He laughed again. "Well, I dunno if I should admit this, but when I met her, a George Jones song popped into my head. She was smooth as whiskey, sweet as wine, and warm as brandy. How could a man ask for more?"

Well, Jillian was all that and more. I told Doc everything. How we met, the tire, the volunteer work, the bet, the dinner, the kiss, and the boyfriend. "It was a pipe dream anyway. How could I expect her to love me? I'm broken. I'm not complete. That damn desert took so much from me, sometimes I wish…"

"Ben, let me tell you something. The moon is only full and complete a few times a month, but there've been countless songs written about it. You are not broken, you're normal—it's just your *new* normal."

For not being my father, or anyone's father, really, he sure was good at it. He always gave me so much to think about. "Well, do you at least have everything you need?" I laughed. *No, because everything I need hopped on a plane bound for Austin a few hours ago.*

"I'm good. Go take care of Rosie and I'll call you next week." Setting the phone back in the cradle, I closed my eyes and tried to picture Jillian and me as an *Us*, but the only image I could visualize was a hunk of cement, dirty and jagged and chipped, sitting next to a sparkling diamond—colorless, flawless, priceless.

I declined the Lowe's offer to spend the rest of the evening at their place. I wouldn't have been good company, so I had just showered, called Doc, and crashed. I'd never begged for sleep like I did the night she left, but I did just that. My journal sat on the little built-in counter I used as a desk untouched, its pages empty. It was the perfect description of me.

There, but not. Alive, but not living.

I prayed I would fall asleep before I fell to pieces. But sleep never came, thanks to the tsunami of thoughts flooding my brain.

The simple fact was, I was in love with her.

And it had nothing to do with sex. She wasn't just a woman to sleep with. She was a woman to wake up to for the rest of your life. What an honor that would be. It sickened me that it belonged to someone else.

When he cornered me in the dining room of the cafe on Thanksgiving morning, he was marking his territory. Jill was his and that was that. He called her 'my friend,' but he was wrong. Friends don't look at each other the way she looked at me, like I was in control of her universe. Gareth Johnson told me he could offer her the world. But if love were stars, I could give her the galaxy.

But could I? Was I enough?

That roadside bomb in Iraq broke me. I completely

fell apart, and no woman needs a broken man. In theory, I'd come home and just like Humpty Dumpty, I'd put myself back together again. I needed to get myself together, before I could love someone else. Only that was impossible. There were pieces missing. I'd left so much in the desert, I didn't know how to rebuild the man I once was. But I knew I could never be enough for Jillian Walker.

I spent the rest of that restless night bouncing between worthy and worthless, but I woke up with a startling realization. I could stop loving her about as easily as I could stop my heart from beating. And I was a fighter, not a quitter. But I needed a plan. However far-fetched, I was going to fight for this. Battling for something unlikely to happen was better than giving up on everything I never knew I wanted.

With a renewed confidence, I walked to the corner store for a newspaper. But the face smiling at me from the front page was a clear indication I'd lost the war before the first shot had even been fired.

Chapter 20

Jill

"JILLIAN, DARLING. It's so nice to see you." My mother lightly pressed her cheek to mine, her definition of affection. In my ear she whispered, "Glad Gareth was able to talk some sense into you." She reeked of Chanel No. 5 and my stomach rolled.

I pulled away, hoping that her scent wouldn't linger on my dress for the rest of the day. "Happy Thanksgiving, Mother. It's not as if Gareth gave me much choice now, did he?" I maintained my friendly expression, but my tone had a bite she couldn't ignore. That was new for me.

She looked me up and down, her face pinched like she'd just sucked on a lime. "The press is here, dear. Did you forget?" She checked her watch. It was white gold and positively dripping with diamonds. I couldn't help but wonder what she'd done to earn that. "Well, we have a few minutes, and Bianca probably has something you could wear."

Ugh. Bianca. My brother Joel married her six months ago. She claims to love him, but I'm pretty sure she's in love with his bank account and he's in love with her silicone implants. That was the only blessing in my accident. I got to miss that gaudy fiasco. There was no way in hell I was letting one stitch of that glorified call girl's clothing touch my skin. I'd rather be naked, and that's saying something, especially now.

"No, Mother, I'm just fine as I am. Gareth wants an all-American girl and that's what the press expects, so that's what they're getting." I brushed past her and into the back doors of the most spectacular house I'd ever seen. And though the house was already brimming with people, I'd never felt more alone.

I stood in the entry hall, standing by *my man*, shaking hands with each person as they left the bar area to eat dinner. Cocktail hour, or *hours*, was officially over and those lucky enough to be deemed worthy were summoned into the dining hall for a feast fit for a king. Of course, in a cordoned off area, tucked into a corner, was a small press crew covering the event. No doubt, my face would be all over the papers tomorrow. When word of Gareth's and my relationship was leaked to the press, they'd done everything shy of breaking and entering to photograph us together. That task had become increasingly difficult since he'd moved to Cambridge. Before yesterday, we hadn't seen each other since the night of my accident. Because of course he'd been too busy moving to Massachusetts to visit me in the hospital… even once.

I was quickly learning that acting would be a terrible career choice for me. Every ten minutes or so, Gareth or my mother would—through gritted teeth and a plastered-on grin—remind me to smile pretty for the cameras. I thought I was doing an okay job, but apparently *they* didn't. I was even getting the side-eye from Gareth's mother, Helena, who eventually whisked me away under the guise of wanting to share a few family recipes with me before we all settled in to eat.

But recipes were usually kept in the kitchen, and instead of turning right, she hooked a hard left and soon we were in her personal office. She closed the door quietly, threw the lock into place, then turned around and leaned back against the cool mahogany.

"Mrs. Johnson?" I was confused. We'd never been close. We'd hardly said a word to each other since her son and I had become official.

"You can stop smiling now, it's just us." She shook her head quickly and a few hairs fell out of her perfect French twist. She crossed the room, soundless on the high pile carpet, and sat on one of the two chairs in a small conversation area off to the side. I followed and sat beside her.

"Everything smells wonderful. I look forward to learning about the family recipes." Awkward? Yes, but I had no idea what was happening.

"I didn't bring you in here to talk about recipes. I wanted to ask you a question." Oh.

"Okay, ask away," I said, summoning a confidence I in no way felt. *Don't ask questions you don't want the answers to.* My mother's voice ran through my mind.

"Jillian, do you love my son?"

Oh. Shit.

"I think Gareth and I will have a happy marriage. We have so much in common and I'm sure that, once we've—"

"That's not what I asked you." She cut me off, but it wasn't hateful. Nothing about her demeanor said she was angry or suspicious. She was asking just as simply as if she were inquiring about finals or if I'd chosen a major. Which I had not.

"I'm not exactly sure what you want to hear." When in doubt, tell the truth, and that was the real truth. But I needed to proceed with caution. I had no desire to let my feelings fall out of my mouth for my future mother-in-law to file away for ammunition later.

"I'll be frank, since we haven't much time. I've been watching you. I don't think you love my son."

I gulped. "I don't know that your son loves me yet, either. I—"

"Let me finish, but please let this stay in confidence between us." I nodded. "I am unable to have children. Of course, we didn't know that until after we were married, so we just decided not to have children. Then, one of Tom's *special friends* fell pregnant. In an elaborate scheme, I was whisked away to a wellness tour of Europe and voila, I returned just in time to have 'my' baby."

"Gareth?" She nodded.

"Yes. He's not mine. There is no part of me in that young man. He was conceived by a selfish bastard and a money-grubbing whore, and every one of their wicked traits were passed down to him." My eyes bulged and my mouth had dropped open at some point during her incredible story.

Helena leaned forward and took my hands in hers. "If I had it to do over again, I would have married for love, and the moment Tom started stepping out, I should have run for the hills." Sighing, she let go of my hands and leaned back, slouching in the chair. It was most unladylike and made me want to hug her sweet neck for the wasted life she'd led.

"I'm sorry," I said, fighting tears. What else could I say?

"Yeah, me too. It's too late for me, but it's not too late for you, ya know." She straightened her spine and smoothed her pretty brown suit, looking more like the dignified lady I knew her to be, rather than an old, washed-up diner waitress.

"But, my father—" I pleaded. It was more complicated than that. Wasn't it?

"No." She stood and now I detected anger. What

the hell, it wasn't like *she* was the one constantly being interrupted. "Don't bring him into it! This is your life and you need to live it on your own terms. I love my husband because I was told to, and in some small way, I love Gareth because I'm supposed to, but that's on me. I didn't make myself a priority and I see you traveling down the same dark and dangerous road. You need to live for you. Tell me about the young soldier you've been spending time with?"

"Umm, I... he's just... " I stammered. This feeling that I'd walked into an exam without having ever seen the material was growing in my gut.

"Gareth keeps an eye on you, especially since the soldier came into the picture. He was displeased that you'd been socializing with him. In fact, he had him checked out, hell bent on destroying him, but you know what?"

I shook my head and reminded myself to blink.

"He found nothing. His records show a sad and lonely childhood, but from what I read, he's overcome great obstacles to get where he is. The soldier is the kind of man you should be with. Not Gareth. And not any other man your parents would approve of." When she smiled, I did too. "What happened to your hand?" She pointed and I looked down. My left hand was turning purple and was definitely swollen.

"Oh, would you believe I hit it on a can of green beans?" I laughed, but sobered instantly at the memory of my last conversation with Bennett.

"It's perfect." She clapped her hands under her chin like an excited toddler. "He was planning to propose at dinner, but he can't now because your finger is too swollen. And a purple hand, ring or no ring, raises questions that no run-in with green beans will satisfy. So he'll have to divert to the original plan and propose in Aspen. It's the only obvious choice."

I nodded, digesting the deluge of information she was throwing at me. "An obvious choice." I had no words, so I repeated hers.

"That gives you less than three weeks to make a decision. And dear girl, pray or meditate or do whatever it is you kids do, but dig deep inside your heart and ask yourself if you're prepared to live the next fifty years with a man who you share no affection with. Because, darling, those fifty years will feel like five hundred." Her bright blue eyes were watery and, without a thought of propriety, I pulled her into a tight hug.

"Thank you," I said so softly, she may not have even heard. She pulled away and held me at arm's length.

"I'll be struck with an unfortunate and ill-timed migraine right before dessert is served. I'll be helped up to bed and won't be back down before you leave." She started toward the door and I'd followed, but she paused with her hand on the polished brass doorknob. "And I mean this in the best possible way. But I truly hope I never see you again." She popped a sweet, grandmotherly kiss on my right temple and swept out of the room, standing tall and proud, a picture-perfect Southern hostess preparing to smile and serve her guests.

Chapter 21

Bennett

KNOWING THAT post-traumatic stress disorder existed, and even understanding what it was, didn't make sleep come any easier. With more free time now that I was no longer educating Princess Jillian about life outside her kingdom walls, I spent it learning more about myself. I'd researched the research, compared study after study, and listened to tapes upon tapes of interviews from soldiers whose experiences made my tour look like a vacation to Disney World.

But when the dreams came hard and fast, within five seconds of my head hitting the pillow, none of that made a lick of difference.

I was transported back in time, held hostage by my own mind as I relived the attack again and again. The horrors of that day were clear, a movie playing on a screen in 3D. How was it so easy to hear the shriek and hiss the missile made when it was airborne and feel the blazing inferno when it made contact?

The putrid stench of charred flesh swarmed around me like

angry bees, making the acid in my stomach churn. Everything within sight was engulfed in flames and my only saving grace was Chance, whose lifeless body shielded me from the catastrophic destruction that fell on all sides. I gagged, almost laughing at the irony that I would survive an attack of this magnitude, only to choke on my own vomit and die because I had a weak stomach.

Each breath became more difficult to draw and I estimated only a few minutes, maybe less, before I succumbed to whatever injuries I incurred in the blast.

It didn't seem right, though. I watched as the men searched; dragging themselves from body to body, using every ounce of energy they had left to check each of the scorched bodies, but none had survived. Who could survive a blast like that? With the men of my unit forever branded by the hate and injustice of war, I watched life as I knew it die in that crumbled desert sand.

"Man, don't take this the wrong way, but I've seen prisoners of war come back looking better than you do right now." Mr. Lowe, or Chance, what he now likes me to call him, just shook his head as he spoke. And he probably wasn't far off.

I ran my hand over my impossibly tired face. "I'd like to blame it on the brutal beating I took from the STAT final I probably just failed, but I looked like this before that." I grabbed one of the tissues I'd stored in my coat pocket to wipe my ever-dripping nose.

"Yeah, I noticed. I stuck some cold medicine in your room and Lillie made a few meals and such for you. I stuck them in your freezer. I hope you don't mind that I went in there, but there wasn't room for them in the break room." I was shaking my head before he even finished speaking.

"No way, are you kidding me? Mi casa es su casa… literally." Chance smiled. I may have tried to, I'm not sure. The head shake had set off a domino effect of pain across the top of my skull and I grabbed the edge of the circ desk to steady myself.

"Go to bed, boy. I'll check on you tomorrow. But don't forget, we're headed out to Arizona on Friday to see Lillie's family."

I may have grunted.

"Yep, I know you're jealous. I mean, who wouldn't want to spend ten whole days with the same in-laws who spent six months trying to convince their daughter that she was too good for him?" Poor Chance. I found it hard to believe anyone could dislike him.

"Well?" That time I did manage a grin.

"Oh, yeah, I totally agree, she's way too good for me, but I needed to get that ring on her finger before she realized it."

The first week of December was known as Dead Week, meaning classes were cancelled and, if you were responsible and studious, you used the time to study for final exams. I tried very hard to be that person, but found myself easily distracted.

"Alright, bed for me. One final tomorrow, then two on Friday. I'll see you."

That night, in my Nyquil-induced coma, I didn't dream about the desert, the missiles, the blood, or the death. I dreamt about Jillian, but that was almost just as painful.

How had I let myself become emotionally attached to someone from another world… one so far away from mine that I'd need one of those NASA telescopes to even see it? She was beautiful, smart, strong as any soldier I knew, and most importantly, she deserved better than the likes of me. Not to say she deserved an ass like Gareth Johnson, but someone in his league. She deserved someone who could give her the life she was used to, someone who could make all her dreams come true. Even a blind man could see that I wasn't the man for the job.

I'd hoped by taking the statistics final on Wednesday, I'd be getting the hardest of the four out of the way early. I'd also hoped, when the stress of that final was out of the way, I'd start feeling a little better. I was wrong on both accounts.

And with Murphy's Law in full effect, on the walk home that evening, the slight drizzle became icy rain.

Gale force winds swept between the buildings, turning the sleet into projectile needles. The day had gone from gloomy gray to dark and sinister in a matter of moments, the temperature dropping dramatically in the process.

But my whole body was trembling, dripping with sweat. I had a fever—there was no debating that fact—and I had for a few days. Just when I thought I was on the edge of death and couldn't feel more miserable, the next day came and proved me wrong.

I was never so grateful as when the front doors to the library came into view through the haze of winter. Every breath felt like a sword was splitting my lungs in two, and at more than one point in the mile-long walk, I'd been forced to stop to catch my breath. The eight stairs leading to the doors may as well have been the Matterhorn, but I set my sights on the book depository at the top of the staircase and soldiered on. I'd get in my warm bed, relax after the bizarre semester I'd had, and go home for Christmas in a few days.

Chapter 22

Jill

MY MOTHER ALWAYS said, *If you fail to plan, you plan to fail.* On that point, we agreed. I was a planner by nature. I always made a grocery list in the precise order of the store before shopping. I always wrote down step-by-step directions before going on a road trip. I wrote them again, in reverse order, before coming home. Vacations were the same way.

But with finals behind me, and Christmas break officially upon me, I found myself staring at my Louis Vuitton luggage, sitting empty on the floor of my bedroom, with no list in sight and no time to make one. I checked the time… 4:00. I needed to leave in three hours to arrive in Austin by midnight. The plan had always been to fly out to Aspen first thing in the morning. As far as I knew, nothing had changed. Packing for the eight-day ski trip should have been my top priority. So, of course, I decided to clean my kitchen.

As I unloaded the dishwasher, my mind wandered to Bennett, as it had so many times in the last few weeks.

The last communication I had from him was a nod toward the doors of the cafe, telling me in no uncertain terms, to stick with what I knew. That one simple action dismissed any ideas I may have had that Bennett saw me as I'd grown to see him. And it still ached like an infected wound.

When I'd run out of distractions, I threw winter clothes and some other necessities into a few bags and loaded them into my trunk. What was wrong with me? I hardly recognized myself anymore. I was going to Aspen! I needed to shake off the pity party. And I had the two-hour drive between College Station and Austin to do it, because in less than twenty-four hours I'd be hitting the slopes.

Great, rain.

The weather mirrored what was in my heart. I ran to the car and jumped in before the rain picked up. With the heater blowing at maximum capacity, I mentally ticked through my 'leaving town' routine.

"Dammit, dammit, dammit." I slammed my hands on the steering wheel with each profanity. There, on my passenger seat, mocking me, was the stack of books used for a report I'd written the week before. If I waited until after the break to return them, they'd be late and I'd have to pay a fine. And when I called in to check my grades, the automatic call-in service wouldn't release them unless my library account was in the clear.

While the former was of little concern, the latter would make my parents none too happy, so off to the library I went.

Desolate roads and darkness, the result of an imminent storm, created a scene straight out of an apocalyptic novel. Campus was a ghost town. The wind picked up, rocking my car, as a slushy mix of freezing rain hit my windshield like miniature buckshot pellets. I prayed it didn't stick on the pavement. I was beyond exhausted and had no desire to creep down the highway, fearing for my life.

After sitting at the curb outside the library doors for more than a few minutes, I had to admit defeat. If anything, the rain was only going to get worse. It was probably best I just bite the bullet, run up the steps, and shove the books in the return box. Leaving the car running, I gathered the books inside my coat and darted for the box. Having to feed them in one at a time was excruciating, and by the last book, I thought I might freeze to death. I laughed inside as another sucker pulled up behind me. Good luck, buddy.

Walking back, the lights from the newly arriving car illuminated the landing of the stairs, drawing my attention to the figure of a man slumped down against a brick column. The devil on one shoulder said, *This is not your problem. Get in your car and go!...* the angel on the other said, *You're better than that, go offer assistance.* As I walked closer, the details once obstructed by the ice-filled air became more clear. And by the time the man was in arm's reach, I had to fight to catch my breath. *That jacket.*

"Bennett?" The man didn't stir. Moving in closer, I nudged him a few times and heard something, a mumble maybe. Okay, so he wasn't dead. The man's face was covered by a sweatshirt hood and pushing it back revealed a nightmare.

"Bennett!" I jumped up and waved my arms to the other guy returning books. "Hey, my friend collapsed! I need help." The scrawny guy came running over and together, we lifted Bennett to his feet. It took every muscle in my body, but we slowly walked him down the stairs. I think Bennett was helping a little, but I couldn't be sure. When it was time to get him in the car, I opened the back door and, with what I know *had* to be at least some help from Bennett, the stranger and I were able to get him in the car. His partial lucidity gave me great hope for when I would have to unload him all by myself.

Beutel, the university's on-site clinic (referred to as the Quack Shack by many) was less than a mile away, but like the rest of campus, it too was deserted. I sighed and rested my head on the steering wheel, trying to conjure up options and failing miserably.

Bennett was sick. And there was no one around to take care of him, which really left me with only one option. "Hang on, Bennett. I'm about to get you dry." I punched the gas and, by the grace of God, we made it home within five minutes and in one piece.

"Hey, help me out here. Sling your arm around my shoulder… " He grunted, I grunted, it was all very uncivilized. "Yes, like that. Now, can you stand?" His legs stiffened and, with a big pull from me, we were vertical. "It's that door right there, just a few more steps." It was slow going, but we made it, both crumpling into a pile on the couch as soon as it was in reach.

Chapter 23

Bennett

The roar of Apaches overhead sliced through the silence, placing me back at the base camp outside of Doha. When I couldn't sleep, I used to try and count each one that flew over, usually giving up after I hit triple digits. Those things were everywhere, fading in and out, like a radio station just out of reach, mingling with the sound of a voice that brought me so much peace.

"No, I owe you nothing, much less an explanation … with this sham of a relationship, with this entire preplanned perfect life I'm supposed to lead. All of it. I'm done being your … don't control me anymore, no one does, so you can go to Aspen or you can go… "

I tried to hold on to the voice, but like the desert wind, it faded away without warning.

It was hot, so hot. God, I hated Kuwait. The mighty desert wind carried with it sand and debris, and grit between our teeth and in our eyes was as common as feathers on a bird. In the distance, the rumble of a convoy grew louder. I had about five minutes before we'd be unloading whatever supplies we'd just picked up from Camp Doha. In search of my squad,

I turned, only to trip and fall to the ground.

"What do you mean, 'I'm going to ruin … If you mean by not marrying … you've got that backward. If you mean I'm ruining your … political aspirations, I literally could not care less."

The voice was angry, irate even, and I felt it like a poison.

"What the hell?" Hot, sticky blood coated my hands and the cause of my fall, a body, lay lifeless in a large puddle of the stuff. Removing the helmet, my heart stopped as I stared into Jillian's lifeless eyes. The cry that escaped my throat was that of a feral animal being eaten alive.

"Hey, sorry I'm … a sick friend. Anyway, I'm not coming to Aspen and I … Gareth. You can have … was always your goal. Good luck with … be very happy together. Talk … Bye."

Night had fallen, and the choppers were gone, along with the threat. "Shhhh… " I closed my mouth and warmth engulfed my soul, creating a peace I'd never known before. It wrapped around my body, chasing away the tortured shadows that had been my constant companions. It tamed the darkness with its presence and I relished in the absence of the torment and despair that had been branded on my heart.

Chapter 24

Jill

SOMETHING CAUSED ME to jump and the book I'd been reading flopped to the ground. My eyes flew to Bennett, asleep in my bed, but he didn't even flinch. Reaching down, I grabbed the paperback and placed it where I'd been sitting. I'd lost my place, but that hardly mattered. In the thirty minutes I'd been reading, I hadn't comprehended a word.

Once I got him inside and out of his sodden jacket, he was dry enough to put into bed, relieving me of the awkward task of wrestling him out of his jeans. I did, however, remove his lace-up Ropers. They'd done a good job of protecting his feet from the elements, so I was able to leave his thick, wool socks in place.

He had been burning up, so I forced some Tylenol down his throat after several unsuccessful tries that resulted in his maroon Texas A&M sweatshirt being soaked. There was nothing remarkable about it, so I cut it off, revealing a thin white tank underneath. I threw the remnants of the shirt on the floor, with the promise of buying him another one at the university bookstore if he'd just get better.

The phone rang and I wondered if that was the noise that caused me to startle a few minutes before. "Hello?" I held my breath. It was several hours past the time I should have been in Austin. My first instinct was to ignore it, but that wouldn't have been fair. All I needed was a search party combing the highway for my dead body, which led me to wonder if there was someone expecting Bennett tonight.

"Jillian, where in God's name are you?" he growled. It was Gareth. Real Gareth, not masked, suave, confident, public persona Gareth.

"You called me at home, so… " *Probably not the best time for sarcasm.* I was in the hallway and I quietly closed the door to my room before heading into the living room.

"Why aren't you here? We fly out in five hours, *Jillian.* We're having to fly commercial and Continental Airlines won't hold the plane, even for me." Wow. That may have been the first time Gareth admitted there were limits to his family's political influence.

"I'm not going." I spoke before I could stop myself, and it wasn't saying those words that caused me to freeze in fear. It was what would inevitably follow when Gareth realized I'd defied him again… and this time, there was absolutely nothing he could do about it.

"Excuse me?" His tone was cool, controlled.

Masked Gareth was taking over. He was equally, if not more, terrifying than the real one because he was harder to read.

"I said I'm not going. My friend is sick and needs to be taken care of." I'd known for a while I'd have to choose. Not between Gareth and Bennett, but between the woman my parents expected me to be and the woman I now knew I was. And I was choosing me.

"You little bitch." Gareth's voice was low and controlled, more terrifying than ever. "Do you have any idea what this trip meant for us? The Kennedys will be there, for God's sake. The press is expecting a headline, *Jillian*. This vacation was strategically planned, and if you think I'm going to let a spoiled, rotten, *damaged* whore ruin my political career to play nursemaid to some insignificant nobody, you're dead wrong."

I flinched, his assessment of me was a slap in the face. He was right, of course. That was a pretty accurate description of the Jillian I used to be, but that girl had been annihilated by the tender heart of the soldier currently asleep in my bedroom.

I sighed, exhausted and preoccupied with worry. "I don't know what to say." I almost apologized, but swallowed it down. I wasn't sorry, not even a little bit, and I was finished with false pretenses.

"How about starting with a damn explanation. You at least owe me that."

"No, I owe you *nothing*, much less an explanation. I'm done—with you, with this sham of a relationship, with this entire preplanned perfect life I'm supposed to lead. All of it. I'm done being your show pony. You don't control me anymore, no one does, so you can go to Aspen or you can go to Hell for all I care!" *Wow, go Jill, go!*

The silence stretched as I pictured Gareth flipping through his rolodex of masks, looking for one that would get him the desired outcome. I took the lull as an opportunity to sneak back in to check on Bennett.

"Jillian... I could have given you the world." Ooh, contrition. Smart move, but not good enough.

"Gareth," I sighed, sitting down where Bennett slept peacefully. The growth on his face, only a few days old I'd guess, was soft under my fingers as I stroked the side of his face. It was time to pull the plug. "The world you're offering is not the one I want." With nothing left to say, I hung up the phone, on my former future husband, on my future life, and on the only world I'd ever known.

Every fifteen minutes, like clockwork, I wiped Bennett's face, neck, and arms down with a cool, damp rag. Caring for him gave me the opportunity to learn the topography of his body. Maybe I should've felt guilt or shame in my exploration, like I was taking advantage without his knowledge. But as I ran my hands along the dips and planes carved into this man by years of hard work, his reaction to my touch was wondrous. His face relaxed, his heartbeat slowed, his breaths became deeper, more substantial.

It's amazing, the way a body can tell a story and the ink on Bennett's arms spoke volumes. On his right arm, an American flag hung vertically, stars to the left, with gentle ripples running through it. Above the flag, in script, was written *No Man Left Behind.* On the bottom half of the flag, negative space created the silhouette of a soldier dressed for battle. It was magnificent.

His other tattoo was simpler, more discreet. Located on the tricep of his left arm were simple lines of text, written in the same scripted font as the opposite arm. It read,

> *I will always place the mission first.*
>
> *I will never accept defeat.*
>
> *I will never quit.*
>
> *I will never leave a fallen comrade.*

It was my new credo. My mission was to help Bennett heal and I wouldn't accept defeat, I wouldn't quit, because there was no way I could leave him behind. Not again. Not ever.

So I continued allowing my fingers to roam, tracing the stars and stripes of the flag, and the words as I read them to myself over and over again. My hands were nomadic, unable to stay in one place for too long. It was all in the name of medicine, I tried telling myself... but 'myself' wasn't buying it for a minute.

When the phone rang again, I was rinsing out the cloth I'd been using on Bennett, so I wiped my hands on my jeans and grabbed the cordless receiver.

"Hello, Mother." I answered, because I knew it. I don't know how, but I knew it.

"Jillian." *Ice queen. It was almost too easy to picture her face: pinched and angular, looking down her nose, dissatisfied resting look etched upon her overly made-up face.* And to think, she'd spent the last twenty years raising me in her image. The thought made me gag.

"Save your breath. I'm not going."
'Yes, I have been made aware. I'm not going to ask you who or *what* prompted you to make this decision, nor will I ask why you've decided to go rogue and embarrass this family, *again*. But... I will say this: If you are not in Aspen within eighteen hours, you are going to ruin *everything*." Wow, that was a lot of power to give one person. *Everything? Really?*

"What do you mean, *'I'm going to ruin everything,'* Mother? If you mean by not marrying Gareth, I'm ruining my life, you've got that backward. If you mean I'm ruining *your* life or dad's political aspirations, I literally could not care less." I laughed, feeling euphoric at giving her a piece of my mind.

"Jillian. I can make things very difficult for you, my

dear." It wasn't a warning. It was a threat. She was cutting the strings tied to my hands, feet, mouth. Because she was no longer the puppet master to my life. Jillian was becoming a *real girl,* just like Pinocchio, and I couldn't be controlled by anything.

I walked back into my room. Ben had kicked off the sheet, so I tucked it back around him, smoothing it across his body, then sat at the foot of the bed.

"You do not want to do this, young lady."

What was her game? I laughed again, quietly so as not to disrupt my charge. She was threatening to cut me off. Well, joke's on her. My grandmother, *her mother,* predicted this years ago and made arrangements for this exact situation, seeing my mother for who she truly was. I didn't need her or my father.

"That's where you're wrong. I do… " I slid my hands down his muscular thighs and he stirred in his sleep. "I do want this. More than anything else in the world."

A nurse, I was not. I was an extremely healthy kid, never really getting even so much as a cold. I'd never felt a forehead to check for fever and I had no thermometer, so I had to get creative. I found by resting my cheek on Bennett's chest, just over his heart, I could answer two vital questions: Was he still alive? And did he still have fever? Checking for the hundredth time since bringing him home, I listened to his beautiful breaths through his shirt, letting the rise and fall of his chest sync with my heart. The situation was status quo. Yes, he was still alive and yes, he still had fever.

Tylenol. It was time for more Tylenol. Though it wasn't doing much good, I grabbed the bottle from the kitchen counter and spotted the phone.

Lori.

I dialed her number, knowing she was about to board a plane, but praying she'd check her messages at some point.

"Hey, sorry I'm whispering. I'm taking care of a sick friend. Anyway, I'm not coming to Aspen and I broke up with Gareth. You can have him now. I know that was always your goal. Good luck with that. I'm sure you'll both be very happy together. Talk later, or maybe not. Bye."

My world had become very small, just a one bedroom apartment, population two—with no ghosts, no pasts, no expectations, no judgment, and no denial. It was freeing.

The second I placed the phone back in the cradle, the screaming began.

Chapter 25

Bennett

MY SENSES RETURNED one by one, creating a series of snapshots, each one revealing more about where I was.

Sound.

I thought I detected voices, but try as I might, I could never catch hold of anything substantial. A ventilation unit kicked on somewhere and there was breathing. The steady rhythm of breathing. Maybe it was my own, but I didn't think so.

Smell.

It was easy to recall the foul stench of war; unwashed bodies, revolting steam rising from MREs, the latrine. But what I smelled was the exact opposite: fresh laundry, clean soap, lavender, vanilla, coffee. It was what I'd expect Heaven to smell like.

Taste.

My mouth was dry, unclean, and a faint bitter taste lingered on my tongue.

Touch.

The thing under me was soft, a warm cloudlike material that molded to my body, taking my shape and cradling me like giant hands. I'd never been picky about where I slept, so long as I was relatively safe. But even if I wasn't, I still slept, just not as well. Extending my hands, the cool fabric under my fingertips was smooth like silk, but there was an unexplainable pressure I didn't recognize. Not uncomfortable though, just foreign.

Sight.

The room was dim, dawn only recently breaking as a silvery diffused light crept through the slats between the blinds. An empty chair sat by the bed I was on and a half-full glass of water sat on the side table beside it. The pressure I'd been confused about was a thin, delicate arm, and while I probably should have flipped out at that point, I didn't, because I knew.

Jillian.

Turning my head, I found myself eye level with Jill's neck. She was halfway sitting up on the edge of the mattress, like she'd started sitting straight up, then slipped during the night. One of her arms was lazily draped over my chest, while the other was behind my neck cradling my shoulder. She was beautiful as she slept, serene, with the face of an angel.

An angel who'd spent the entire night with her arms

around me.

I stared at her, committing the image to memory, when her eyes fluttered open. Immediately she smiled, but like a switch had been flipped, her smile dropped away and with wide eyes she jumped up, extracting her arm from underneath me.

"I'm sorry, but... " Her voice was too loud. She looked up at the ceiling fan, then down at the comforter, anywhere but at me. She took a calming breath. "You were screaming. I tried waking you, but you tugged me down beside you and it made you stop, so I stayed." Night terrors. *Damn it.*

Using my wobbly arms to push myself up, I sat and reached for the water, only then realizing I'd been stripped down to just my undershirt. I looked at my chest and bare arms, trying to see the emblems of my military life through her eyes, the ink on my skin just another reason I would never be enough for her. When I looked back up, she was staring and a wrinkle had formed between her brows.

"You had fever. I think you still do." She took a step toward me, then hesitated. "I had to cut your sweatshirt off so I could cool you down." My heart slammed against my ribcage. What else was gone? I took a peek under the sheet covering me, grateful my jeans were still in place.

"I need the bathroom," I croaked. And I did. Bad.

"Oh, right through there." She pointed. "Do you need help?"

Then she stepped back and covered her mouth. Her face turned twenty shades of red, realizing what she'd said. "I meant from here to there, just getting down the hall, not... " I shook my head, willing myself not to laugh. I secretly loved the perma blush she often had around me. I wonder if *he* also held that honor?

The man staring back at me in the mirror was unrecognizable: sunken cheeks, purple-rimmed eyes, hair sticking out in all directions. And the smell, good Lord, how could she stand being so close to me? That thought brought up feelings I was not ready to contend with.

"Do you mind if I shower?" I attempted to yell from behind the closed door.

"Nope, go for it." Her answer, almost instant, was loud. Had she been standing right outside the door?

"Thanks."

I made quick work of washing up, but stayed under the water until it ran cold.

Why was I here? What had happened? And where was *he* during all this? Because there *was* a he, wasn't there? A powerful, off-brand Kennedy wannabe, who acted as if he owned her. The man who sought me out in the dining room of the cafe, when everyone else was occupied, to make one thing very clear—Jillian Walker belonged to him and him alone, and that I was to stay far, far away starting now. Who also assured me that he had the influence and was fully capable of ruining me if I didn't comply. Then he made sure to throw in that I was yesterday's trash, and that she only had eyes for him... had for years... and by Christmas, there would be a ring on her finger to prove it. *Oh yeah,* I thought, *then why have I never heard of you before now?* But he was right about one thing. I was trash and she deserved so much better than a damaged man with a darkened heart.

I cut the water off and grabbed a towel. It smelled like her, too, of course. Everything did. I should leave. Redressed in the same clothes I'd gone in with, I opened the door. Jillian was sitting on the couch, but popped up as soon as she saw me.

"Is everything okay?" I nodded, feeling water drip down my back from my still wet hair that needed to be cut a few weeks ago. "Do you want me to take you home?"

Without warning, the room started to spin. I swayed, reaching out to steady myself against the door jamb and almost missed it completely. Jill rushed to my side.

"I've got you," she assured, but her words were strained. I leaned heavily on her as she helped me back to bed, knowing I would fall without her support.

"Sorry." I grunted.

"I'll take that as a no." I nodded, unable to speak under the effort.

Vertigo was the worst. I'd gotten it a few times in Kuwait when the temperature hit 120 degrees and the water was too hot to drink. I detested my tendency to get dizzy when dehydrated, but I'd never been happier for it to strike. With all talk of my going home abandoned, I let her help me back into her bed.

Her condo was nicer than what the majority of college students lived in. At least, I imagined it was. Decorated to the nth degree, there was no doubt anyone but a gorgeous girl like Jillian laid her head down here. Her walls, painted the palest of lavender, almost grey, were sparsely adorned with framed pressed flowers, each having the scientific name handwritten below in loopy script. The bed, which sat higher than average, was made of cherry wood, as was the rest of the furniture. It was very tidy, and looked almost unlived in. A set of perfume bottles over here, a stack of books placed neatly over there, and a framed picture of Jillian and a younger adult male that looked a lot like her. They were both smiling at the camera with Kyle Field, Texas A&M's football stadium, in the background.

I lifted my legs into bed when she pulled the floral comforter up, granting me access. As soon as I was settled, using giant, pastel-colored pillows to cushion my back against the wooden headboard, she covered me from the waist down, fussing to make sure things were situated just right.

"So, dinner? I made you soup. And by 'made,' I mean I opened the can, added water, and heated it up in the microwave." The tiniest of grins graced her lips. That squeaky clean face, free of makeup, paired with her casual, collegiate running pants and T-shirt, made her appear so young and innocent. She was getting to me, so I closed my eyes to combat her womanly wiles. It did me no good. The image of her standing beside me in maroon and grey cotton was as clear as day. I tried imagining latrine duty or mucking horse stalls, palpating cows. Anything to get my mind off the girl less than a foot away. I needed to end these feelings.

"Yes. Thanks." I looked down, smoothing my covers until she left the room and I could breathe again. I used the seclusion to inspect more of her bedroom. It could have been a magazine feature, the way everything was arranged so perfectly. From the woolen blanket casually thrown over the upholstered, overstuffed chair in the corner… right down to the matching coffee mug on the table beside a giant paperback book with a clock and a kilt on the front. Noticeably absent though, were any pictures of Jillian with *him*. I wondered where he was right now, while his girl was tending to the needs of a dirty boot unchaperoned.

I don't remember Jillian ever coming back in with the soup, only waking up with an untouched bowl of chicken, noodles, veggies, and broth sitting on the side table and a not-pajama-clad Jillian laying next to me, her body wrapped around mine like a vise.

Chapter 26

Jill

IN THE WHOLE of my twenty years, I'd only had eyes for Gareth Johnson. Because my parents said so. Sometimes I wonder if my parents whispered his name to me in my sleep to fuel my ambition to make him mine. Once I turned sixteen, I was put on The Pill, then shipped off to Texas for a long weekend each month, tasked with winning his heart. Because my parents said so.

Looking back, a scrawny, underdeveloped high school junior gaining the attention of a college freshman who lived several states away should have been quite the challenge. But it was not. I did what was expected and we were pronounced a couple after a few months. And I was happy, because I was told to be. This would be a diplomatic fairy tale, the marrying of two political families who would become the new hope for the Republican party, now that Reagan's term was over.

I loved him because my parents said so, but that wasn't love. Love couldn't be prescribed. It couldn't appear at will, nor could it disappear on command. Love was something that grew from a carefully planted seed. In its own time, in its own way, love bloomed for all to see and, if nurtured, love could stay lush and beautiful for a lifetime.

I knew this only because that seed had been planted in me. I'd felt it grow for weeks and weeks. But love could be a lonely journey. Because it didn't take two to love. And love could only truly thrive if the feeling was returned.

Rejection wasn't a word I was familiar with. The idea of loving someone who didn't love me back was foreign. And the pain associated with it was indescribable. My heart was a gaping wound and having to care for Bennett, knowing he chose to send me away on Thanksgiving, was like pouring salt right into it.

"Bennett?" I called to the man beside me. I'd slept beside him all three nights he'd been with me, in an attempt to keep the terrors at bay. Most of the time his calls were unintelligible—sometimes names, places, commands. But this time, he yelled my name. Over and over again, he yelled my name, revealing a crack in the cold, aloof armor he insisted on wearing to distance me. "Bennett!"

He flailed, sweat pouring from his brow. His hair was dripping, and often he'd moan, squeezing his eyes tight when he did. I'd done all I could and I couldn't heal him. It was time to call in the experts. I found the phone on the kitchen counter and, taking a deep breath, dialed 9-1-1.

Chapter 27

Bennett

I'D RESIGNED MYSELF to the fact that, as long as I stayed with Jillian, I'd wake up with her arms around me. Should I mind? Yes, I should. Very much. Did I? Hell, no. But did it make it near impossible to freeze her out while awake? Yes, yes it did. Still, her touch in the darkness was more welcome than she could ever know.

"Ouch!" What the hell was happening to my arm? Was Jillian squeezing me? And why? My eyes flickered open and I turned my head as a blood pressure cuff continued to strangle my arm.

"Oh, hey! There you are! Welcome back, hon." An older woman, dressed in light blue from head to toe and round all over, whispered, looking up from her task. She finished writing something on a clipboard before unfastening the cuff from my arm, the sound scraping against my eardrums, which had become accustomed to gentle silence. "I know someone who sure will be happy to see those pretty golden eyes of yours." She nodded to my other side as she exchanged an empty IV bag for a full one while I watched on, wordlessly, trying to figure out where I was, why I was here, and who she was talking about.

I turned to look around, pain shooting through my neck and head. I found Jillian seated in a padded chair, bent at the waist using my arm as a pillow. She was sound asleep, but had a firm grip on my non-IV hand, so I used the other one to stroke her head. I could feel the rhythm of her breaths on my arm and she looked like she'd been crying. She was perfection.

"She rode with you in the ambulance and she's been right here ever since, refusing to leave your side even for a minute." My throat constricted and I wondered… "Good thing, too. Those are some mighty hairy dreams you've got playing in that head of yours, but luckily she knew how to calm you right down." I leaned over and placed my lips on the top of her head. Perfection.

The chatty nurse placed the clipboard in a slot at the foot of the bed and came around to place a white blanket across Jillian's shoulders. She stirred, but didn't wake. "You're a lucky man, you know. She sure loves you a lot."

I cleared my throat to speak, sending more bolts of pain through my head. With that, Jillian raised her head and dropped my hand as soon as she saw I was awake. "Hey." Her sleepy voice was one of my new favorite sounds, but I'd never let her know it.

"How long have I been out?" Tone steady, face clear of emotion. I'd been trained to make myself unreadable. This should be second nature.

"About twenty-eight hours." She said, checking her watch. She ran a hand through her hair, smoothing it down but making no difference at all, other than being adorable.

"Why am I here?" I uttered huskily, needing to clear my throat, but unwilling to try again after the pain that shot through my head the first time.

"I couldn't get your fever to come down. It was out of control and I didn't... " She covered her mouth and took a few shaky breaths. "I thought you might... that you might not be okay, so I called an ambulance. You have viral meningitis."

Meningitis was serious, I could easily have died. I hid my shock and tried to maneuver my body higher in the bed. Jillian handed me a corded control that allowed me to raise the bed to a sitting position. She reached out to touch my face, but I flinched, so she stopped. I was afraid one more touch would be the end of my resolve. "I feel better." *Lie.*

"Good." She swallowed and looked away.

"You don't have to stay here and mother me." I closed my eyes, not wanting to witness the effect my cold words would likely have on her.

She breathed in deep, letting it out slowly. "I'm

not here because I have to be Bennett. I'm here because I—"

"Stop." Just like in the kitchen when she wouldn't leave me alone about spilling the hot water all over me. The word echoed in the silent room and I pinched my eyes closed tight. "Look, I think you've got the wrong idea about this. A year ago, maybe I'd be up for some fun and games, but that's not for me anymore. I'm not that man anymore."

She sniffed. She was crying, and my will was slipping, like grains of desert sand through my fingers. "You need to leave my room. Now." I turned my head away from her and closed my eyes again, waiting. Her initial footfalls were slow, hesitant even, but gained momentum the closer she got to the door. Within a few seconds, I was alone again, the way it should be. It was the right thing to do. She deserved so much more than I could give her.

Chapter 28

Jill

THE SOUND OF SILENCE settled between the walls of my home like a poisonous gas ready to smother me. I could have turned on the TV or the radio, but I didn't. I would gladly be smothered, rather than feel the pain I was experiencing. His absence was a living, breathing thing… like another person occupying the space with me.

I'd been sitting on the couch for minutes, hours maybe. I had no clue. The sun was starting to set and I'd arrived home midmorning. I had yet to face the bedroom, knowing that seeing the spot where Bennett had slept, still holding his shape, would choke me.

The phone ringing from the kitchen was the first sound I'd heard in hours.

"Hello?" It was weak. I was weak. I was missing a part of me.

"He's agreed to take you back." Fresh tears hit my cheeks at the enormity of everything.

I just couldn't.

"I don't want him back, Mother." I was exhausted and it sounded like it. At that moment I realized the sun wasn't setting... it was rising.

"Don't be ridiculous. What's gotten into you, that you're willing to give up marrying a Harvard Law graduate, with a family as important as the Kennedys—if not more—and enough wealth to pay off the national debt? Tell me, for what?" She clicked her tongue when she was finished and delivered a deep, 'woe is me' sigh.

"For love, Mother." I shook my head. It was something she knew nothing about. She couldn't honestly think I believed she and my father were in love. I think they respected each other, but outside the public political arena, their lives couldn't have been more separate if they lived on different planets.

"We have been over this, Jillian. The love will come, but the power behind a pairing like yours and Gareth's is like nothing this country has ever seen. He *will* be president some day. That is a fact. He was groomed to take the office, just as you were groomed to be by his side." She was frantic. I couldn't remember a time my mother had ever been out of control.

"That's not what this is even about... I can't marry Gareth. I just can't."

"That makes no sense, Jillian. Why can't you?" She was grasping, but as she always said, *Don't ask questions you don't want the answers to.*

"Because, I'm in love with someone else."

Then deafening silence, the kind that physically presses on the ear.

"Well... " She cleared her throat to mask her emotion, finding her balance once again. "You are *not* the daughter I raised." That made me laugh.

"Thank God for that!" Call waiting beeped and I switched over to the other line without so much as a goodbye.

"Hello?" Then, seconds later, I replied to the caller on the other end of the line. "I'm on my way!"

Chapter 29

Bennett

"WELL, MR. HANSON, it looks like this will be an easy discharge."

"Easy, you say?" Nothing about this was easy, as I sat staring out the picture window that faced five or so other medical buildings. The sun had set, then risen again, and my condition was stable. But the new day did not bring new hope. Because I was still me and she was still her. And she would always deserve more than I could give her.

"Yes, sir. Everything has been taken care of so just sign here, and here, then we'll get you out and back home... just in time for Christmas, too!" And with that, another hundred pound weight fell on my shoulders. Christmas. I told Rosie and Doc I'd come home. I'm sure they've been expecting me and are worried sick. I was just so tired of disappointing everyone.

"Wait, what do you mean *taken care of*?" I asked, as I waited, impatiently, in the wheelchair they insisted I ride down in. The same chatty nurse from the day before said she'd call a cab and I assumed it was on its way. I was perfectly fine to walk, though. I never again wanted to be viewed as fragile, but she wasn't having it. She made it clear that it was against hospital policy to let me walk out on my own and if I wanted to leave, there was only one way out. And I *wanted* to leave, that was for sure.

"Oh, the bill dear. Someone settled your bill." She used the table by the bed to neaten her stack of paperwork I was to sign, but I shook my head and made no attempt to take it from her.

"I think there's been a mistake."

She flipped through the paperwork, a line forming between her brows. A slight frown settled on her face as she skimmed the half-ream of paper in her hands.

"Nope, no mistake." The voice came from the hallway, but soon she was standing right next to me. The nurse and she exchanged looks and Nurse Chatty smiled, clipping the papers back onto the board. I closed my eyes and breathed through my nose.

Jillian.

Why was she here? She refused to look at me. "Thanks for getting him ready, Barbara, but I'll take the patient from here."

I shook my head. "I'm not going home with you." I looked toward the nurse for support and repeated my statement. "I'm *not* going with her."

Chatty's knowing smirk grated on my nerves, like

this was all some big game to her. Clearly, Jillian had an ally in the older woman. "Well, I don't rightly care where ya go. Alls I know is, ya can't stay here."

The woman bounced out of the room and down the hall, the squeaks of her shoes becoming faint before disappearing all together. When she was good and gone, Jillian wheeled me out into an unfamiliar corridor. I must have come in this way, but I certainly had no recollection of it.

Jillian pushed the down arrow and we waited in silence, but once we were in and the doors were closed, I looked back at her. "I am *not* your hostage." My teeth were clenched, and a whole new level of headache radiated between my ears.

"Oh, yeah? Well, I have paperwork in my bag that sings a different song. You've been released into my care and in my care you will remain."

As if on cue, the doors to the elevator opened, and she pushed me out into the freezing cold air. "Damn it!" Oh, I was mad, and since she'd cut my shirt off I was still in a paper-thin scrub top and pants made of coffee filters. I had half a mind to jump out of the chair, but really, where would I go? And how would I get there?

Finally, we stopped beside her car. "Why are you doing this?" My roar seemed to have zero effect on this girl. A year ago, I could make a private pee his pants. I was losing my touch.

"What does it matter?" She opened the passenger door and held it open expectantly. "Why can't you just let me help you? Why are you making everything so difficult, fighting at every turn?" Then she started muttering about me being a prick and needing to get my head out of my ass. It would have been hilarious if the wind hadn't been whipping through my clothes and I wasn't so pissed off about my kidnapping. I stood on shaky legs.

"You need to back off, woman. This is not what I need." I was not even two inches from her, yelling, in her face. Nothing, not even a flinch. She was about as scared of me as she would be a butterfly. I couldn't decide if I loved her or hated her for that.

"Oh yeah, jackass? Well, I think this is exactly what you need. Now, get in the damn car." I may have actually jumped at her roar. The girl could be scary when she didn't get her way. But, getting in her car and out of the cold made good sense, given my condition. It by no means meant I was conceding.

Jillian rolled the wheelchair back to the lobby and returned seconds later, started the car, and drove out of the hospital parking lot without so much as a glance my way.

I assumed she was taking me home. I'd been waiting for her to ask for my address, having no idea what I would say. The library? I wasn't even sure it was open, being this close to Christmas. If not, I was screwed. I had nothing but the shirt from my back when Jillian found me and now that was cut to shreds.

"Where are you taking me?" My head was back against the headrest and my eyes were closed.

She looked at me, right in the eyes. "Home Bennett. I'm taking you home."

Chapter 30

Jill

COLLEGE STATION WAS still a ghost town, so the drive home took less than ten minutes. I'd taken great care to ease around corners and into stops, hoping to keep Bennett as comfortable as possible. Turning into the parking lot of my condo community, I saw it was basically deserted, too. Given it was three days before Christmas, it wasn't surprising. People who had a home (and were speaking to their parents) went there for Christmas. Then there was me.

"This doesn't look like my home." He hadn't even opened his eyes. I don't know why he was being so difficult. I was almost positive he didn't have a home, so I decided to test my theory.

I threw the car in park and turned to face him. "The way I see it, this is the closest thing you've got to a home, so suck it up." His eyes popped open. Yep, I hit the nail on the head with that one. Bennett was homeless, living in the library I'd guess, but that could be sorted out later. I had more important things to worry about.

He was slow to get out of the car, and even slower getting up to the porch, but he refused my help each time I offered, *stubborn ass*.

No sooner had I opened the door than Bennett, in an impressive show of renewed strength, plowed through and headed straight to the shower. So predictable. It was his escape, the one place he knew I wouldn't go to confront him. Well, he was wrong. I wasn't giving up and if he didn't come out, I was going in.

I wondered what he thought when he walked in and found the clothes I'd grabbed for him. I had stopped at Target after he kicked me out of his hospital room the day before and braved the last minute Christmas shoppers to make sure he'd be comfortable once he came home. I'd been pretty thorough, purchasing T-shirts, sweatpants, socks, and boxers. I stood on the aisle with the soap and bodywash, smelling every bar and bottle they had, trying to replicate the clean, piney scent that always lingered on his skin. I must have looked like a fool, especially when I found the right one and jumped up and down a few times. Hopefully he'd find that on the counter, where I'd also left him a comb, deodorant, and a toothbrush.

Now that I had him, I planned to keep him.

I put a Stouffer's lasagna in the oven, then decided to tackle the mess in my bedroom. I hadn't come this far into the house since the EMTs rolled Bennett out on a stretcher, and it needed a once-over. It probably needed more than that, but from what I knew about Bennett, once the water started, I had roughly ten minutes.

I ripped off the old bedding, throwing it in a pile by the door. I had a spare set, so I'd wash it later. The exact moment I grabbed the spare sheets from the linen closet, the bath water started on the other side of the wall, quickly followed by the stuttered spurt of the shower. My heart was beating post-cardio fast and I ran back into my room and wrestled with the fitted sheet. I heard movement, and once I think he elbowed the wall, making me jump. I pulled the top sheet up and yanked on a new quilt just as the water cut off.

My shaky legs bounced with each step as I walked back into the kitchen. My breaths were fast and my heart beat even faster, waiting for him to come out. Why was I so nervous?

Lucky for me, I didn't have to wait long. He stepped out of the steamy bathroom, hair neatly combed, and completely dressed. His pants hung low on his hips, loose enough for that casual, *I'm not trying* look, but tight enough to highlight the strength in his muscular thighs. He'd pulled on a grey T-shirt, the closest I could find to the army shirts I was so used to seeing him in. On his feet, he'd pulled on the thick, white socks.

The sight of him made me want to cry. I couldn't believe he was here. Watching him being carried out on a gurney, so pale and lifeless, put me face-to-face with the possibility he may not recover. And now he was standing in front of me. And grumpy or not, I couldn't help but appreciate the beautiful, broken man standing in front of me.

He'd been running a towel over his damp hair, but he stopped when he saw me and then stomped into the kitchen. He insisted on banging every cabinet door during the process of looking for a glass and when he found it, he filled it from the tap and I heard him drink it all down in one gulp. What was meant to make me mad just made me smile and I was glad the couch faced away from the kitchen where he couldn't see me. He was acting like a child and I found humor in that, but he didn't need to catch me laughing at him.

"Take me home." He was behind me and I stood to face him, the couch a barrier between us like a line in the sand. But he was underestimating me. Because once a girl realizes she deserves better, she's relentless in her pursuit for what she wants. And I wanted the man standing in front of me.

"And by home, you mean… the library?" I crossed my arms over my chest, waiting for an answer. But when his jaw clenched, and his shoulders dropped, I'd have given anything for a do over.

"Look, I'm sorry." I rushed around to his side of the

couch. Reaching for his hand, I tried to explain. "I didn't mean—" But he recoiled at my touch. *Which was just mean.*

I stood there, frozen in shock, the events of the last days, weeks, months even, swirling around in my head. Finally, I just asked.

"What the hell is your problem?" The closer I came to him, the more he backed away. It was like a slow-motion cat and mouse chase as he circled around the couch to escape. But I was quicker and met up with him on the other side. This wasn't nearly over.

"Look, I don't have a problem. I just—" His sigh was deep and rocked his whole body. It was heartbreaking. He looked defeated, like the first time I saw him walking out of Mrs. Lowe's office... what seemed like a lifetime ago.

"You just what, Bennett?" We were in a standoff and I wasn't backing down without an explanation. "What did I do to make you treat me this way? Why are you being like this?" I was choking. This wasn't, at all, going according to plan. "Why won't you let me touch you?" Because that's what I wanted. I wanted to touch him. I wanted to make him feel better. I wanted to help him and be a part of his life. I wanted... him.

"God, Jill." He ran his hand through his freshly combed hair, mussing it up into something even better. "Why can't you just see that I'm not good enough for you?" The pain in his eyes almost brought me to my knees. *Is that what he thought?*

"*You?* Not good enough for *me?*" I looked around, ready to put an end to all of this. It was time to air the dirty laundry and he was going first. I grabbed a long, black umbrella from the coat rack nearby. "Is it because of this?" I used the metal tip to lift the hem of his shirt, exposing the burns I'd caught glimpses of while caring for his fever. He stood like a statue, his jaw and fists clenching in time with one another.

"Or is it because of this?" I reared back and hit the shin of his right leg as hard as I could with the umbrella. He lost his balance for a fraction of a second as the sound of the umbrella hitting whatever he was hiding under those pants echoed through the house. His eyes got wide and he stared at me, like I'd lost my mind… and maybe I had.

"You've got scars. And you're missing a leg. So?" Tears poured down my cheeks at the emotional outburst and the relief it brought just to get this all out. "What makes you think you're so different?" He wasn't moving, wasn't speaking. I was scared I'd broken him. After a few beats, he slumped down on the couch.

"Jill, I'm not—" I stopped him with my hand. I wasn't ready to hear it. What if this was it? What if this was the last time we were together? What if he walked out of this place and never looked back? I couldn't bear the thought. I closed my eyes, struggling to gain control. But not for too long. Because if these were the last moments we spent with each other, I wanted to remember everything.

"Everyone has scars, Bennett."

"No." He shook his head, looking straight up at me. "Not everyone. Not you. I'm not even a whole man and you... you're perfect." I gasped.

"Perfect?" A maniacal laugh slipped from my lips. "You want to see perfect?"

Chapter 31

Bennett

JILLIAN PUSHED ME back on the couch and stood directly in front of my knees. She was so close, I could reach out and touch her, but I held back. She seemed to have more to say. Never breaking eye contact, she reached up and slowly started unbuttoning her shirt.

"Jill, what are you doing?" I reached up to stop her, but she shook her head. She had calmed down, her tears had stopped.

"I'm showing you *perfect*." With the last button free, she turned so I was looking at her back. With one quick motion, she shrugged, and the shirt slid off her shoulders where it fell in a puddle at my feet. I stole a glance at her skin, flawless with a light dusting of freckles across her shoulders. I wanted to touch her. I needed to confirm she was as silky smooth as she looked from where I was sitting. But I didn't get the chance.

Calmly and with the grace of a dancer, she turned back around, revealing angry red, webbed skin on her right side and across her torso. "How's this for perfect?" she whispered.

And it took just one flick of her wrist behind her, and the pretty pink bra she'd been wearing came sliding down her arms, uncovering even more of her hidden secret. The burns continued, covering her entire right breast, stopping just below the shoulder.

"Jill, no, stop," I demanded and tried to grab her hands as she tugged on the button of her jeans. "I get it."

She backed up, placing herself just out of my reach. "No, I don't think you do, Bennett. I'm just getting started." She wiggled her narrow hips and her oversized jeans fell down, pooling around her ankles, before she kicked them away. Jillian Walker stood in front of me, wearing only a small pair of pink panties, and I couldn't breathe. Tearing my eyes from her body, I met hers and saw they were brimming with fresh tears. The burns extended all the way down to her knee and a giant, red surgical scar covered her hip and lower torso. It took every ounce of willpower I'd ever been given not to cross the two feet that divided us, but I knew this had to play out on her terms. I sat on my hands to keep from touching her.

"My volunteer work at the cafe was not altruistic by any stretch of the word. A few months before, I'd driven drunk and run my brand-new little sports car up a telephone pole in the middle of the night. A Good Samaritan pulled me out of the burning car moments before it exploded, but not before leaving me… like this." She turned 360 degrees to show me everything.

"See, Bennett." She sniffed. Tears freely streamed down her face as she looked at me. "You're not so special. We all have scars." With both hands, she wiped the tears from her face, but more took their place almost immediately.

I looked her up and down while she watched, taking in the details of the body my imagination had dreamed of more times than I could count. Never, in my fantasies, had she looked quite like the reality that stood before me.

"But I was right," I simply stated. Her brows knitted together, and she cocked her head… as if that would help her understand.

"Right about what?"

I leaned forward and placed my palms on the backs of her thighs—pulling her close, planting my lips on her right hip—and kissed one of the worst scars on her body. "You. Are. Perfect." I pressed my head against her stomach, directly on her burns, and almost instantly she cradled it, running her hands through my hair. It was perfect. Everything about the moment was absolutely perfect.

We stayed like that for I don't know how long. I didn't want to let go. Because I'd done it. I got my mind set straight and I'd gotten the girl I never thought would give me a second glance. She was mine now. She was in my arms, holding me against her like I was the most precious thing her hands had ever touched. I pulled away just enough to look up into her beautiful eyes. Eyes that didn't just look at me, but *saw* me.

"These aren't scars, Jill." I pulled, yanking her down onto the couch. She landed in my lap, facing me. "They're wings." Her hands continued their assault on my hair while I ran my hands up and down her perfect imperfections.

"I don't understand… " She looked free, like she'd just rid herself of the world's burdens as her lips connected with my forehead.

"These scars… they brought you to me." Her breath caught and I wrapped my arms fully around her, bringing her beautiful body flush with mine. "But you *were* right about one thing. I am homeless." Jill pulled back and we found ourselves nose to nose. She shook her head back and forth, so very slowly.

"No, you're not." She grabbed my face between her hands and pulled my lips to hers, but just before they met, she whispered, "Not anymore."

Chapter 32

Jill
March 1993

I LOVE SLEEP. I love it maybe more than ice cream. And alarm clocks are the devil. But when the alarm clock comes as a twenty-two-year-old hunk of muscle with soul-searching eyes and a smile that could light up the world—*and* he smells like bacon—waking up after a long and leisurely holiday from school wasn't so bad.

"I am seriously going to grow out of all my clothes if you don't quit cooking all the time." I kind of meant what I was saying, but it's less convincing when accompanied by a cheesy grin and grabby hands stuffing the delicious breakfast into my mouth as soon as the last word comes out.

"Cooking for you is the very least I can do, Jill." Bennett was sitting on the edge of the bed with a tray full of bacon and waffle sandwiches, a thing that wasn't a thing until we made it a thing. Because that's what we did. We took two pretty incredible things and paired them together to make them even more amazing. It's what we did with each other.

"I have to go. I've got class and then my last day of training at the counseling center." I'm positive that pride beamed from my eyes. I still got chills thinking about how Bennett was approached about a job counseling veterans who were now students. Because *who better* to help them work through the mess in their heads than someone who'd been there and done that?

"I have a study group, so I'll just have to meet you at the cafe." Talking with my mouth full was probably not the most attractive thing in the world, but that's one of the many things I loved about Bennett—he loved the good, the bad, and the ugly of Jill Walker. I still felt completely underserving of his love, but I was working on it. Every day I worked on replacing the narrative ingrained in my head by my parents with the new story I was writing with Chance and Lillie Lowe, my new friends at the cafe, and of course, my boyfriend, Bennett.

After that cold December day when we shined a light on all our truths, we never spent another night apart. And that was a good thing. The heart bursting with love and a lifetime of kisses I'd been saving up… I now know were meant for him. Sergeant Bennett Hanson—my roommate, my best friend, and the man I hoped to spend the rest of my life with.

"Hey, you said you'd reconsider our sleeping arrangements once we got back from spring break and well, we're back… " I let my voice drift off. While it's true we never spent another night apart, Bennett spent his actual sleeping hours on the couch. Because of course, in addition to being gorgeous and brave and sensitive and funny and probably the most intelligent person I'd ever known, he was also honorable.

"I really have to go. Can we talk about this tonight?" I nodded, a little disappointed. We *would* be talking about this tonight. "Good." And he stood, then leaned down to kiss me goodbye.

"Ewww, no," I squealed, as I turned my head, throwing my hands up to cover my mouth. "Morning breath."

A roll of his eyes, a shake of his head, and a kiss on the hair, and he was gone. I fell back against my pillows with a face-splitting grin, wondering how I got so lucky.

Chapter 33

Bennett

THE NINE HOURS I had to spend away from Jill felt like nine hundred, but eventually I was boarding the bus from my new job at the counseling center, headed for the cafe. Jill was still in class and would be for the better part of another hour, but I still really needed to hurry.

"Is everything ready?" I called into an empty dining room the second I walked in the door, but I didn't have to. My sense of smell told me what I needed to know. I busted into the kitchen and stopped short. Lillie and Chance stood at the stainless steel island in what looked to be a standoff. Clearly, I was interrupting something big.

"Hey—" I said, when they both looked my way.

"Boy, we need to talk." Lillie's hands flew to her hips and she cocked her head to one side, daring me to defy her order.

"Woman, you need to leave that boy alone." Chance turned to me. "My lovely wife here is having cold feet by proxy."

I took a few more steps into the room, walked right up to Lillie Lowe, and placed my hands on her shoulders.

"I'm listening. Say your piece." I knew what was coming.

"Are you sure you know what you're doing?" Her pinched brows were so sincere and my heart swelled with love for these two people whom I now considered family.

"No, I don't. But when I was in the second grade, I pushed Brooke Kirby on the swings every day for two weeks before asking her to be my girlfriend, and you know what? She said no, because one time the year before I got a better grade on a spelling test than she did." I sighed, wondering what ever happened to that uppity little girl. They both just stared at me.

"That makes no damn sense." Lillie was hacked. I'd never heard her cuss before.

"Yeah, it does, baby… " Chance glided around and wrapped his big arms around his wife. Their size difference was just unnatural and I didn't think I'd ever get used to it. "Because even if things don't go his way, he's still a winner. It takes bravery to walk into something terrifying, unsure of the outcome. The boy's got guts, you've got to give him that." He checked his watch and tilted his head in the direction of the back door.

"Lillie, my instincts have never failed me." She glanced down at my leg, then cut her eyes back at me. "That doesn't count. My instincts knew exactly what I was getting myself into, but I did it anyway. I have a good feeling on this one... plus, what's the worst that could happen?"

"She could say no." I swear there were tears in her eyes.

"She could," I agreed. "But I got through it once, I'll get through it again." I gave her a wink and headed out the back door.

As usual, I heard her before I saw her.

"I'm so sorry I'm late." And then a few seconds later, "Just let me get my apron." Followed by, "Where the hell is my apron?" Sometimes that girl could go from sweet to pissed in the blink of an eye, especially when it came to that goofy apron. "Grrrrrrr." I heard her growl, before another muffled response, then, "Outside? Why would it be outside?" She yanked the door open to find me standing by the dilapidated picnic table. I'd managed to use a few wood scraps from the job site down the street and some screws to temporarily stabilize it. But there wasn't much I could do to fix a table that had probably been around since Texas was its own country.

"Looking for this?" I pulled her apron from behind my back and her face instantly softened. Still standing in the doorway, she took a small step back when she spotted the picnic basket.

"Bennett? What's going on?" She was side-eyeing the table, then shifting back to me. That happened a few times before I laughed out loud.

"Do you believe in love at first sight, Princess?" I asked, holding my hand out to her. Reluctantly, she closed the few feet between us and took it. I guided her over to the table and we sat just as we had four months ago, on what I secretly considered our first date.

"No, but I believe in *annoyance* at first sight." She chuckled at her own joke, and I did too.

"I'm starting to think those two things go hand in hand." And I pulled her hand, the one I was still holding, to my lips and kissed her knuckles.

She tipped her head to one side, no longer laughing, and stared into my eyes. "What's this about, Bennett?" Her voice lacked the confidence that had been bred into her. She was worried.

"A few months ago, we spent a few hours out here, just talking and getting to know each other. And that night, as you dropped me off, you thanked me for sharing my story with you."

A soft smile graced her face and she nodded. "I remember like it was yesterday."

"Well, there's more to the story, and I'd like for you to tell me how it ends." She held my gaze for a long time, different emotions flashing across her face.

"How?" she asked. She'd scooted so close, our knees touched. It was the most intense eye contact I'd ever been a part of and solidified this life-changing and somewhat sudden decision even more.

"Jill, I came to Texas A&M to heal, but that didn't really start until I met you." She drew a sharp breath and shook her head with conviction.

"No, Bennett. There was never anything wrong with you. If anything, you healed me." I scooted closer to her on the bench. She was practically in my lap.

"You have no idea, do you? You have no idea that, before you, I was battered and broken. And I'm not just talking about my leg, I'm talking about all of it. My mind was trapped in the hell of my past, my soul was haunted… my perspective was completely twisted. But, when I was with you, I could breathe again. My heart remembered to beat. You did that for me. First by pissing me off, then by trusting me. You gave me a purpose."

"And what purpose was that?" I'm nervous, like the heart-pounding kind of nervous. All of the sudden, I feel like I'm about to take the first step down a dangerous, uncharted road, completely unarmed. Because, how do you prepare for your heart to possibly be torn from your body?

"To be the kind of man who deserved the kind of

woman I knew you could be."

"Bennett... " But I held up my hand. I wasn't finished and if I didn't say what I came here to say, I may never be brave enough to try again.

"I'm a simple man. I can get by with practically nothing, you've seen that. I wanted for nothing, but then I kissed you, and it was like we just clicked into place. Now, there's something I don't just want, but I need."

"What?" She scooted into my lap and wrapped her arms around my neck, sitting higher, so I had to look up at her.

"Us. I want us. And I want it forever."

Her mouth crashed down onto mine and I held her so tight, I could feel her heart beating against mine. Pulling back, the broken connection was almost painful, but this was it. I stood, swinging one leg and then the other, over the bench, and pulled her up to do the same. Once we'd untangled ourselves, I pulled her in for one more kiss, then carefully, got down on my left knee and held out my open palm, which contained a simple gold band that housed a modest diamond.

"I am about as far away from Prince Charming as you'll ever get, but I want the rest of my story to be, *and they lived happily ever after*. So, Jill Walker, will you marry me?"

Chapter 34

Jill
May 1993

SUMMER IN TEXAS was literally hot enough to bake cookies on the dashboard and fry eggs on the sidewalk, but a Texas spring is what made life worth living. And our wedding day didn't disappoint.

The chapel on campus was small, but it was all we needed. On the groom's side were Rosie and Doc, Bennett's foster parents and partners in the ranch they now owned together. And on my side were Lillie and Chance Lowe. Our friends from the library and the guests from the cafe were spread equally between the two sides. I hated they had to pick a side at all. We were all one big family.

I checked the clock. Twenty minutes. A knock on the open door made me jump. "Ms. Walker?"

"Yes?" I knew this woman, but I couldn't place her for the life of me.

"You may not remember me. We met about a year ago. You were a guest in my courtroom." The older woman smiled and so did I, as I walked to her and took her hand.

"Judge Kirby, I can't believe you're here." She laughed.

"Well, to be perfectly honest, Lillie Lowe called me. We're old friends and I've been keeping tabs on you. When Lil casually mentioned you were getting married and needed an officiant, I stepped up."

"I guess that explains why she all of the sudden said she had it covered." I chuckled, fiddling with the satin edge of the beautiful vintage veil Bennett and I had found at an antique festival in one of the neighboring towns. That was something we loved doing together: turning other people's trash into our treasures.

"I don't feel like you're the same girl who stood before me a year ago." Hand on her hip, she was looking me over with a skeptical eye.

I nodded. "That's probably the best compliment you could give me." Looking back, I hated the person I'd been before. That petty, egocentric girl didn't deserve Bennett Hanson and, more than anything in the world, I wanted to be worthy of his love.

"And I hear wonderful things about this man you're marrying. You really are a completely different person, aren't you?" Her soft smile said she approved of the woman standing before her. I nodded again.

"Thank you, not only for being here today, but for

your tough words the last time we spoke. It may have taken a while to sink in, but you were right. About me, about my attitude. Everything."

"Well," the judge said, smoothing her grey pantsuit, picking off a piece of imaginary lint from her leg. I think my praise made her uncomfortable. "I guess I better get into place. But Jillian, I want you to know, I don't regret letting you off with a pathetic slap on the wrist." She grinned.

"That pathetic slap brought me to the love of my life." She tipped her head with a quick nod and walked out the door. My heart was so full.

I checked the clock again. Ten minutes until the ceremony and Bennett promised to come in beforehand. I'd made the request knowing I'd lose it the first time I saw the man I loved in uniform.

"Jillybean?" I spun around as Jerome and Nanny B entered the bride's room.

"Oh my gosh, I didn't think you were coming!" I could hardly breathe at the sight of the two of them. They exchanged a look I'd need to investigate, but for now, I was just so damn happy to see them. My parents had marked the invitation *Return to Sender*. Not that I was really surprised. They were appalled that I'd ejected their dreams from my head and had chosen to follow my heart.

"We wouldn't have missed it for the world,

especially since I'm close personal friends with both the bride *and* the groom."

Wait. What?

Then I heard footsteps unique to Bennett. "Biscuit! Mrs. Botts! So glad you made it!" Bennett rounded the corner, clapping Jerome on the back. "It sure is good to see you!" I wanted to razz my future husband for keeping such a big secret and ask him how he'd connected the dots, but I had no words.

It was hard to believe the man standing in front of me, with his magnificently tailored suit and his shiny brass buttons, was the same man who'd come to the cafe for a free meal six months before. It was even harder to believe that in just a few minutes, he would be my husband.

"Wait, *you're* Biscuit? Now I feel like a complete idiot." I heard his momma call him Biscuit from time to time, but I thought it was because he ate biscuits and sausage gravy with the same frequency most people drank water. "From everything Bennett's told me about his buddy, Biscuit, from the hospital, I can't believe I never connected the dots." I shook my head, choking back happy tears as Bennett caught my eye over Jerome's shoulder.

"I love you," I mouthed, words spoken from my heart to his and meant for no one else to hear. He stepped further into the room and collected me in his arms.

"And I love you." He whispered into my ear, sending sparks throughout my body. He was perfect. *Absolutely perfect.*

"Miss Jillian?" The woman came toward us and I grabbed her tiny, curled hands in mine.

"No, it's Jill. Just Jill from now on, okay?"

The woman nodded, a soft smile gracing her lips. She was getting old, it was hard to deny, but she had the same spark she had back when the three of us were running around the estate together. I looked to Jerome and knew he felt what I did; the gaping hole where CJ should have been.

"I've got you, girl." Jerome said, patting my back a few times. I nodded, trying and failing to stop my tears as Jerome pulled out a framed 8x10 picture of CJ, looking so smart in his uniform. I would have given almost anything to have him by my side. "Now, I know it's not the same thing, but how about I set this up right beside me in the church. He would be thrilled to see how happy Bennett makes you." He turned to face my groom, but something was terribly wrong. Jerome's face fell. "Hanson, man… you okay?"

Bennett looked like he'd seen a ghost. "Who is that man?" His wide eyes filled with tears and, with no shame whatsoever, slid down his cheeks.

"This is CJ Lacey. He was our best friend growing up. He came to his grandma's house every summer and the three of us did everything together." He knew the stories, because we'd spent hours talking about our childhoods, mine more than his. He knew more about CJ than he did his own parents. Bennett took the picture from my hands, pressed his head against the glass, and completely lost it.

"Ben?" I was running every possible scenario through my head to explain what was happening, but I came up empty. I'd tried to learn all I could in the months since we'd been together about Post-Traumatic Stress Disorder, and for a moment, I thought the soldier in the picture had triggered some memory.

"Chance James."

I looked at Jerome, but he just shrugged, as baffled as I was about Bennett's odd mood change.

"That night when you were telling Raf about your two best friends, you said that CJ never told you what the letters stood for. It's Chance James. We usually went by our last name out there. I was always *Hanson*, but he hated his—said it sounded too feminine—so we just called him Chance. We met in basic. Went all the way through together. We were two halves of one whole."

No one knew what to say or where to look. It was like someone pushed pause in the room and we all just stood there, waiting for someone to unpause us. But there wasn't a dry eye to be found.

"He saved your life." I knew the story, almost as if I'd been there too. With the help of Paul, his pseudo counselor, Ben finally told me what he saw in his nightmares. I'd never tell him, but I sometimes had the same nightmares after hearing about the horrors he witnessed. The human mind wasn't made to handle such tragedy.

"He threw his body over mine and took the brunt of it." His tone was so somber and as he spoke, he looked at nothing and everything all at once. "If he hadn't been there that day… if he hadn't done what he did… I'd be dead." This was a lot to digest five minutes before walking down the aisle.

"Nobody better ever try to tell me there isn't a Jesus. This is a miracle, right here." Nanny B wiped her eyes with a hanky and pulled Jerome out of the room to take their seats, leaving us alone.

Bennett's face was drying, but he wouldn't meet my eyes. He was scaring me. It was like he had something else on his mind, but didn't know how to say it. "What is it?" I'd come up behind him and laid my head between his shoulder blades. Sometimes, just getting close to him was enough to pull him out of the darkness.

"There's something I—" He turned to face me. "This is you, isn't it?" He handed me a scrap of paper he'd pulled from his wallet. Taking it, I smiled, bigger and wider than I had in my life.

"Yes, that's me. We took that with my new Polaroid camera right before he left one summer." The photo was worn, torn, charred in places. I could see why the person smiling at the camera was hard to recognize. I handed it back.

"He carried this picture with him wherever he went, always in his shirt pocket, right over his heart. He'd always tell us when he got back he was going to marry that girl one day, even if he had to take her kicking and screaming."

That made me laugh. It was something I'd heard a time or two as well. "It was never like that with CJ. We were friends, only ever friends." I thought back to all the times he'd asked me out and all the times I told him no. It wasn't just because of Gareth, either. I just didn't feel for him what he felt for me and I hated that for him.

"You were his Golden Girl." *That broke my heart.*

"No, Bennett. I was never anybody's anything until now. From almost the very moment we met, I've been yours and yours alone. No one else has ever had a piece of me." I wrapped my arms around his midsection. "I promise marrying me isn't breaking some best army buddy code." He continued to look at the picture, but at least that put a smile on his face.

"Speaking of getting married, are you about ready to become Mrs. Jill Hanson?"

That was easy. "More than anything else in the world."

Chapter 35

Jill
October 1999

IF WISHES WERE HORSES, beggars would ride... isn't that how the saying goes? It was true though. I could throw pennies into fountains all day and wish on every star in the sky and not ever get the one thing I'd wanted since the first time Bennett Hanson placed his lips on mine.

I stirred the pot of spaghetti sauce, letting my soul take a breather from the whirlwind of emotions I'd experienced over the last few days. I gasped when big, strong arms snaked around my waist from behind, pulling me out of my fog.

"I was gonna go grab a shower, but this smells way too good. I just realized I'm very hungry." Bennett's words—practically growled into my ear as he rested his chin on my shoulder—sent sparks coursing through my veins. Because he'd buried his nose in my hair and pulled my body tight to his, I was fairly certain he wasn't talking about food.

"Down boy." I used my hip to bump him away. "I'm hungry for food and dinner will be ready in about twenty minutes. Go grab your shower, let me feed you, and then... who knows?" I cocked my eyebrow, faking enthusiasm. Bennett was trying, bless his heart. I knew he felt the same way I did, but instead of feeling sorry for himself, he was trying to get me out of my funk. But I was heartbroken. And nothing could ever fill the now permanent hole in my heart.

He spun me around and pulled me into him, cradling my head to his chest with his big hand. He knew that wrapping me tight in a full body embrace was an effective way of getting my mind off of reality. We stayed that way for several minutes as he fluttered kisses on the top of my head. "I love you, Jill. Nothing will ever change that. And Dr. Polasek didn't rule out the possibility completely."

"Ben, her exact words were, *With the damage to your uterus as a result of your accident, it is highly unlikely you will ever get pregnant.* 'Highly unlikely' is, like, one step away from ruling it out completely." I tried to pull away, but he wasn't having it. So instead, I burst into tears for the hundredth time that day.

"Shhhh, baby. There are so many other options. And we're so young. Please don't cry." I sniffed and used the bottom of his T-shirt to dry my face. I hadn't bothered to wear makeup in days. Why, when I'd just cry it off?

"I'm sorry I'm such a mess." *Sniff.* "It's just… all of the disappointment when I find out I'm not pregnant each month added together and multiplied by a thousand couldn't even come close to what I felt hearing Dr. Polasek's words." *Sniff.* "I want to be a mom. I want to make you a dad. There are people all over the world *accidentally* getting pregnant and having children they don't want and it's just not fair." *Sniff.*

"I know, baby. Why don't we make an appointment with that agency Marian told us about? Let's just see what they say." I nodded, but my heart wasn't in it. Not yet. I needed to mourn my loss before I could move forward. Isn't that what Bennett always says when he goes into psychologist mode? "I'll run upstairs and grab the pamphlet she gave us. Be right back." He smacked a sloppy kiss on my lips and ran up the stairs while I got back to my poor spaghetti sauce before it was beyond saving.

Knock, knock, knock.

I jumped. Looking to the stairs (where I just knew Bennett would appear), and then back to my spaghetti sauce (which was almost decidedly burned)—I debated what to do. A second set of knocks got my feet in motion and I headed for the door.

"Hi, Jase," I said, upon seeing the face of our sweet next-door neighbor. "I talked to your mom a little while ago. She called to let me know you'd be alone tonight. Is everything okay?" He nodded, but he didn't look like himself, so I motioned him in and he followed me to the kitchen. Maybe if I added a little water I could salvage this sauce.

Jase lingered in the doorway, looking as nervous as a whore in church. "I'd like to talk to y'all about something... personal." His voice cracked. He was adorable. "Do you mind if I sit down?" I nodded, then called for Bennett, who came pounding down the stairs almost immediately.

"Hey, Jase, what's up, man?" The two shook hands and I noticed Jase's were shaking.

"So," he cleared his throat. "I have this friend at school and... she's homeless." I couldn't help the gasp that escaped my lips. And the concern on Bennett's face aged him ten years. He took a seat beside Jase and nodded for him to continue.

"I don't know the whole story, but I do know she needs a place to live, like yesterday. Her mom died a few months ago, and she doesn't have a dad."

I thought the lump in my throat might choke me as I tried to control the sting behind my eyes. The silence was heavy, like a weight pressing on my heart. This conversation right here—the one my husband and I were about to have with this sixteen-year-old boy from next door—carried with it the air of change, but I couldn't quite wrap my head around what I was feeling

"What she needs is a family." My head snapped to

Ben when he said the words, because that's exactly what I'd been thinking. He looked up at me, eyes bright, and I could see the deep rise and fall of his chest. He felt it too. But the crease in his brow said he was worried.

"Look, I know you're approved to be foster parents. I was hoping, maybe, she could stay here until… " His words faded away and he was looking at the hands he was wringing in his lap. I could see the rise and fall of his chest too.

I suddenly felt the need to keep busy, so I got up and checked the sauce. I think the water did the trick, so I turned off the burner, before addressing Jase again. "Where has she been staying since her mom passed?" I didn't even sound like myself.

"Well, she's been hiding out here and there… I don't really know. I… um… " He stammered and wiped his hands on his jeans. It was becoming clear why he looked just like an alcoholic caught with a case of beer.

That heavy feeling was gaining weight. "Do you think she'd like to meet us?" Bennett asked the question, then shot his eyes in my direction. They said, *Is that okay?* And I hoped my smile replied, *Hell yeah.* God, I loved that man.

"Um, yeah, I think she'd like that a whole lot." Good I thought, because we would too. Jase's wide eyes and deep *Oh, shit* sigh confirmed what Bennett and

I were both thinking.

Ben laughed. "I assume she's at your house right now? That would explain why you look like you just broke out of prison." I wanted to assure him that his secret was safe with us, but my husband was one step ahead. "And no, we won't tell your mom. Just bring her over, will you?" *Do not cry, do not cry, this could be nothing. Do not cry.*

"Sure. Let me go get her." He stood and headed for the door, but stopped. "I want you to know," Jase said as he turned back toward us. "She's just my friend. There's nothing inappropriate going on at my house."

Ben and I both nodded and I may have fibbed a little when I said, "It never even crossed our mind." With a smile and a wave, he was out the door and Bennett and I both released breaths we'd been holding for what felt like forever.

Chapter 36

Bennett

WORDLESSLY, I STOOD and started a pot of coffee while Jill arranged the cookies and brownies she'd brought home from the bakery on a pretty plate. All of that took about ninety seconds and after about a minute, the *tick- tick- tick* of the kitchen clock became too much.

"Jill," I warned. "I need you to take some deep breaths. I'm not sure what's going on in that pretty little head of yours, but whatever it is, you need to pack it away before that girl walks in here. This could be something, or it could be nothing... and I don't think going into this meeting with expectations of any kind is healthy."

"But—" Tears were welling.

"No buts, baby." I grabbed the coffee pot and placed it on the ceramic trivet she'd placed on the table for just that purpose. "We are about to meet Jase's *friend*." I emphasized the word 'friend' because something in the boy's eyes told me there was more to it than that, plus we were in need of a little comic relief.

Jill smiled. Mission accomplished. "Let's see the situation for what it is and see what happens from there." She nodded.

We heard a little knock, and Jill practically teleported to the door. "Come in, come in." She tried to smile her tears away, but the emotion in her voice made it hard to mask what she was feeling.

Jill entered the kitchen first, followed by one of the most beautifully exotic faces I'd ever seen. She looked as though she could've just stepped out of a 1970's disco movie, with her wide, expressive eyes and head of unruly black hair. I hadn't really envisioned an image of Jase's friend, but even if I'd done it a thousand times, it could never have been as breathtaking as the little broken bird standing in front of me at that moment.

"Becky," Jase began. "Let me introduce you to Jill and Bennett Hanson. Jill... Bennett... meet Rebecca Johns. She goes by Becky." I took her tiny, little hand when she offered it, but when she did the same for Jill, she was pulled into an unexpected embrace that both melted my heart and hardened it all at once. Because I knew what was going on in my wife's mind. And the likelihood of anything coming of this was depressingly low.

"I'm sorry," Jill told Becky, quickly swiping under her eyes for errant tears. "I don't know what came over me. Can I get you something to drink?" A nervous Jill was a chatty Jill, and while I should have probably jumped in to save her from looking frazzled, it was just too precious to stop. I hadn't seen her this happy in a long time. And even if it lasted only five minutes, it would be worth it.

"I'd love some milk, ma'am." The girl's words were shaky and I hoped it was nerves and not fear to blame. Jill had a tall glass of milk on the table before I could blink and Becky thanked her, then looked at Jase with disbelieving eyes. I was a pro at reading people, and this girl wanted to know what the hell she was doing here. She was on the verge of falling apart, I could tell.

""So, Bennett and Jill are certified with the state of Texas as foster parents, which means—"

She sighed. "I know what that means, Jase." She turned her gaze to Jill and me, as we both just sat there staring at her, like freaks. "Sir, ma'am, Jase has designated himself my own personal superhero. He's swooped in to save the day for me a lot lately. I'm sorry that he's bothered you tonight, but I'll be okay." She took another deep breath. "You don't have to—"

Jill rocketed out of her chair with so much force, it tipped backward and landed on the tile with a loud bang. "Please, don't go." And everything I'd just been thinking about Jill's five minutes of happiness being worth it flew out the window. I was about to witness my wife's already broken heart shatter into a few more jagged pieces. Her wild eyes moved between the two teens sitting at our kitchen table. "Please… " She reached out and placed her hand on Becky's arm, then looked to me for backup. *Please don't let her leave*, her face said. *Please.*

"Rebecca, we have a guest room," Jill started. "Heck, we have *three* guest rooms, and Bennett and I... " She giggled, then looked at me for approval, which I automatically gave. "We would be happy to let you live with us until... well, I don't know how to end that statement. Forever, I guess. I mean, if you want to... "

A comment like that should have set off all kinds of warning bells and red flags. *Red alert, red alert, wife is in danger of utter and complete destruction.* But it didn't. Because I could read Becky Johns like a children's book. This girl was alone in the world and scared to death. All she wanted was to feel safe and loved. And while there's a laundry list as long as a football field of things my wife and I *can't* do, loving this little girl wasn't one of them.

We were all awkwardly standing by then. Becky stood to leave, Jill stood to stop her, Jase stood to stop Becky, and naturally, I stood because I'd spent enough time sitting after the bombing. Becky took a few steps toward us and asked a simple, yet haunting question. "Why would you want to do that? You don't even know me." Her unkempt hair and face free from makeup, added to her small stature, gave the illusion she was ten or eleven and not sixteen. It was hard not to think of her as a child. But she wasn't one. She was practically an adult.

"Well," Jill twisted a small towel in her hands, while she thought. The poor thing would be torn to shreds by the end of the night if I didn't save it. "According to your superhero here, you're a child with no family. Is that correct?"

Becky nodded, her eyes like wide pools of deep brown, fringed with long, thick, black lashes. Jill reached for my hands before adding, "And we're a family without a child. It seems to me the puzzle pieces fit." The words hung in the air like the sweet scent of honeysuckle on a warm, summer breeze.

Becky turned to face Jase, giving the tears that had been balancing on her eyelids all night permission to escape. "Was this the plan you mentioned earlier?" He nodded and she closed the gap between them, hugging him so tight I'd have feared for his life had his smile not told me he was exactly where he needed to be. The Papa Bear inside me—something I didn't know I even possessed—started to stir. I tucked my wife in under my arm, hoping against hope that this story would have a happy ending. If not for all of us… then at least for the sweet girl clinging to her *friend* like a lifeline.

Finally Jase, the sixteen-year-old voice of reason, explained that letting her stay with us immediately might be frowned upon by child services. But his mother, a family law attorney, would be home tomorrow—and at that point, we could make a plan to have Becky legally placed in our temporary care. Reluctantly, we agreed. What the boy said made perfect sense, but this whole *spending the night with boys* thing was over once she became ours.

And really, who was I kidding? She was already ours. We'd claimed Becky Johns the second we laid eyes on her because she was the answer to years and years of prayers. All we ever wanted was a child to love. And to become parents. We were already asking for so much, I didn't think we had the right to be picky about the packaging.

After saying goodbye, we crawled right into bed, dinner completely forgotten. Pulling my wife into the crook of my arm, I whispered, "Are you happy?" I felt her warm tears on my bare chest, but in spite of that, she nodded.

"She's already mine. I know I'm setting myself up for an epic heartbreak, but I just can't help it. When I hugged her, she became mine."

"You mean *ours*, don't you?"

She lifted her head just enough to meet my eyes and I looked down my nose at her. "What?"

"She's not just yours, baby. She's *ours*." Jill slowly nodded, a soft smile danced across her lips, before settling back down on my chest.

"There's only one problem with that though… " I cocked my head. I'm sure there were about a million problems we'd have to tackle before she could truly be ours, but I wondered which specific one she was talking about.

"What's that, babe?"

"I think she may already belong to Jase Pearson." She giggled when I growled.

Sure, Jase Pearson was one of the smartest, most well-mannered kids I'd ever met. And he already looked at her like he'd personally change the rotation of the earth if she asked him to, but I wasn't quite ready to admit that. Because I wasn't sure he was good enough for my girl.

Chapter 37

Bennett

March 2013

"YOU PROMISED TO TAKE me to Scotland!" Her face was beet red, all twisted and scrunched up. I grabbed a cloth and wiped her brow.

"Breathe, sweetie." Jill's intermittent whimpers ripped my guts out. Her pain was my pain, but it would be over soon enough. "I promise I will take you to Scotland for our twenty-first anniversary." A single tear escaped and slid down her tired face. "When I promised to take you for our twentieth, I had no idea you'd be pushing a human out of your, well... body." One corner of her mouth turned up. She wanted to laugh, I know she did.

"Oh, oh, oh. Here comes another one!" She grabbed my hand and attempted to break every bone in it at once. "Where. Is. Becky?" She grunted. Once the contraction passed, Jill was able to relax again, but I knew it was short-lived.

The door to the delivery room flew open with a

bang. "Momma?" *Oh. Thank. God.* My savior.

I left Jill's side and met Becky at the foot of the bed, behind the nurse in her catcher's stance. "My beautiful girl, your mom and I sure are glad to see you!" I hugged my daughter, pulled her close, and whispered, "Your mother is possessed. Proceed with caution." One quick nod told me she understood.

"Hey, Mom, I'd say you look great, but... "

"Incoming!" Jill was able to give me about twenty seconds of notice before a contraction ripped through her, just long enough for me to grab her leg and help her any way I could. Becky, never one to be shy, grabbed her other leg as my beautiful wife strained and panted and pushed. The lifetime of heartache she'd endured up to this point was hard enough, but now, the pain at seeing her dream become a reality slayed me. We'd waited twenty years to meet this child and that moment couldn't come soon enough.

"Stop pushing, stop pushing. We're about to have a head." Jill's eyes got huge and her face paled. Becky burst into tears while the nurse popped her head out to call the doctor.

"Mom, listen to me. Focus on my words. When I was struggling in soccer and wanted to quit, you said, *Your body was built for this.* When I was in labor pushing Cash out, and said I couldn't do it anymore, you said, *Your body was built for this.* Both times you were right. And, Mom, you may not have believed it before this moment, but your body was also built for this."

The second Cash made his entrance into the world nine months earlier, kicking and thrashing like a baby pig, Bec passed the torch to her mom. "Do you remember what else I said, Mom?"

Jill nodded as she winced in pain. What were they *doing* down there? I didn't really want to know, but Becky was distracting her like a champ.

"I do. You said, *Okay, Mom, now it's your turn.* It was the first time I truly believed I could carry a child."

"And here we are, nine months later. Coincidence? I think not." Bec popped her head up and looked me straight in the eyes. "Grab her leg Dad, this is it."

"Okay Jill, I'm going to ease the head out, then ask you to stop." Dr. Polasek, the one who told us to never lose hope, was about to hand us our masterpiece. "When I do, you have to stop so I can suction the baby's nose and mouth, then find the cord. When I tell you to push again, that'll be it."

I kissed my incredible wife on the forehead, even more in love than the day I married her. When we heard a set of awfully healthy baby lungs screaming, there was a collective sigh. Our family of three had just become four. From somewhere below what I called the human equator, I heard, "Do you want to meet your baby?"

Jill sat up—holding my hand on one side and Becky's hand on the other—while tears coursed down her cheeks. So many prayers, so many wishes, all wrapped up in such a tiny little bundle of wrinkles and squeaks.

Squeezing my hand she smiled, and with a shaky breath, she simply said, "More than anything else in the world."

Our modest living room was bursting at the seams, full of all the people we loved. Rosie and Doc were in from the ranch. Lillie and Chance, now retired, drove down from College Station. And of course our cul-de-sac neighbors, Claire and Kyle Clark, and Marian and George Preston were all there too.. Their children and grandchildren ran around the house with our granddaughters, Whiskey and Ruby Grace.

This was the same crew, minus a few newcomers, who were here the day we were officially able to say, *It's a girl*. That was the first time, by the grace of God, Jill and I became parents. Becky's adoption felt like a lifetime ago. It was now one of the two happiest days in our lives.

I stood next to where Jill sat on the couch and she handed me our little pot roast-sized baby, all wrapped in white. I cradled him in my arms and kissed his fuzzy little head. He was our miracle and he was ready to meet the world.

"First, thank you for coming." We'd kept the sex of the baby a secret for two days, just long enough to get home and gather everyone in one place. "When Jill and I started our lives together a little over twenty years ago, we pretty quickly learned it was highly unlikely that we would ever conceive a child. So, as you know, we did what any sane, newly married couple would—we adopted a teenager." The room burst into applause and laughter as I shot my eyes at my oldest.

"Thanks, Dad," Becky answered, in that deadpan way she had. The roaring crowd died down.

"Today, we'd like to introduce you to our son, Bennett Chance Hanson. We'll be calling him Chance." I passed my son to Rosie, his grandmother, knowing full well I wouldn't see him again for a while. But how could I begrudge anyone wanting to love on my boy? My hands were empty, so I jumped on the opportunity to take a breather and grab my wife a drink.

Casey Clark and his wife Vaughn made their way over to where I stood in the kitchen, away from the crowd. "Congrats again, old man." Casey slapped me on the back.

"Thanks." I looked around to make sure I was alone with the couple. "And thank you again for not spilling the beans about Chance." Much to my surprise, I'd run into Vaughn and Casey in the hall at the hospital the day Chance was born. I told them I'd only let them see the baby if they swore to keep the gender a secret. And if they told me why they were floating around the floor dedicated just for babies, looking like goons.

"And your news, I suppose I should be offering you congratulations as well... when do you think you'll share?" Just mentioning their news turned them into goons all over again and I couldn't think of a more deserving couple.

"Soon. Really, really soon." Vaughn hugged my neck and the two rejoined the crowd.

"So, Grandpa?" Whiskey, my beautiful granddaughter, breezed in and threw her arms around my neck, hanging on to me like a monkey. "Do you want me to go find whoever has Chance and steal him back for you?" Her devious smile was the carbon copy of her mother, in body, mind, and spirit. I nodded, not quite ready to go back into that crowd, but wanting to see the little person who made me whole again.

"More than anything else in the world."

Acknowledgements

So, I've affectionately named this book The Beast, though I'm really not sure why. Probably because, right smack in the middle of writing this baby, I was offered my dream job. And while it has been the most incredible, life changing experience, it was leaving the comforts of what I'd been doing for twelve years and diving head first into a completely new world, new climate, new culture, and new language. All of that to say, poor Jill and Bennett stayed simmering on the back burner like a long forgotten pot of spaghetti sauce.

I was thrilled when things settled down and I was able to get back to what I love. As always, my family has been amazing through everything. Through ups and downs, they're always there, cheering every step of the way.

Huge thanks go to Kate Bihm and Kara Comte for legal advice (for Jillian, not me!), Carrie Merrill for her medical expertise, Nathan Wolf for giving me his writer's and soldier's perspective of things, and Dawn Husted, a fabulous author and critique partner. My dedicated beta reading crew, Carrie, Kim, Leila, and Kristen, came through for me once again! I'll never be able to thank you for your insight!

Scars Like Wings is my fourth book, but my first under my incredibly dedicated and insightful new editor, Christie Scambray. Props to Christie for cleaning up my messes, not only in Scars Like Wings, but meticulously combing through my other three books to fix mistakes that should've been caught before publishing. This girl is not just an editor, she's been my partner through this crazy summer of major transition and can't wait to see what the future holds for us.

And to the man, the myth, the legend.

Your presence is felt in every male lead I write.

Ladies, he does laundry, he grocery shops, he cooks and often serves me dinner when I'm lost in the world of writing. He charges my devices, takes the kids to soccer practices, feeds the dogs, puts gas in my car, buys me tacos, loves me unconditionally... And he's mine :)

About the Author

CHARLY STAGG IS WIFE to one lucky guy, mother to four incredible kids, and teacher to hundreds of children in her community. A graduate of Texas A&M University, Charly holds a degree in Elementary Education and taught first, second, and third grades for more than ten years before getting her dream job as an elementary art teacher. She is a lover of reading, soccer, camping, Aggie football, 90s rock, and all things creative. Her writing process includes typing in bed, while snuggling with her doggies and listening to Goo Goo Dolls with an endless supply of Sonic drinks and ice cream on hand. Charly and her husband live in College Station, Texas with their four children: Andrew, Ryan, Grace, and Lucas, and two dogs, Daisy and Pepper.

Coming Spring 2018

Life on the Ground

A FAIRY TALE LIFE
BOOK 5

C. B. STAGG

Made in the USA
Middletown, DE
20 August 2022

71860352R00183